MEMORIES OF THE WAY IT WAS

Alene Veatch Dunn

Copyright © 2017 Alene Veatch Dunn

Photograph for Front Cover by JRDunn Photography, Jasper, Texas.

All rights reserved. No part(s) of this book may be reproduced, distributed or transmitted in any form, or by any means, or stored in a database or retrieval systems without prior expressed written permission of the author of this book.

ISBN: 978-1-5356-0920-3

DEDICATION

This book is dedicated first to my late husband of almost forty-four years, George Dunn. He always encouraged me and believed in my writing ability. He went to his heavenly home in 2010, leaving me with many wonderful memories. Second, to the two most special sons anyone ever had, Jeff and Jason Dunn. They make me proud, and make sure I'm doing well and behaving myself. Third goes especially to my two granddaughters, Allie and Olivia Dunn, who give me so much joy. I hope these stories will help them to understand their roots and the people from whom they came. Thank you all for the joy you bring to my life.

CONTENTS

Dedication iii
Remembering Manor Hill 1
All Day Singin' And Dinner on The Ground 7
Bob White 11
Callie And Elmer 13
Cecil's Story 17
Chores And Day's End 23
Country Churches 27
Daddy Built A House 31
Did She Or Didn't She? 35
Forgotten Terms 39
Granny's Old Safe 45
Hog-Killing Day 49
Houses Of The Past 53
Love Makes It Real 57
My First Vacation 61
Neighbors – An Old Concept 65
Politics And Election Night 73
Singing Birds 77
Sleeping Porches And Dog Trots 79
School Days 84

Seven Little Faces	86
Spring Time	88
Summer Place	90
Uncle Chester And Aunt Vie	91
Uncle Lonnie And Aunt Artie	95
Uncle Matt And Aunt Hattie	99
Tales Of The Chicken Yard	105
Thanksgiving Of The 1940s	107
The Battle Of Nournberg (Nuremburg)	111
The Hands	114
Wagons, Slides, Horseback, And Walking: Transportation Back Then	117
Washday On McKim Creek	123
Washing Dishes Way Back When	129
What? No TV? No A/C? No Electricity?	133
What I Learned From My Daddy	137
What I Learned From Granny Worry	141
What I Learned From My Mother	145
What I Learned From Papaw Worry	149
Summer Place	152
About the Author	153

REMEMBERING MANOR HILL

Author's Note: Many readers may have lived in a house at a little farm like this in your childhood. Many of these memories will open up your mind to things not thought of in years. This is the tale of the little farm at Denning, Texas, where my maternal grandparents, Willie and Evie Rains Worry, lived and farmed. It is the place where I learned so much about life and how to live. Open up your heart and you will have "memories of the way it was."

MY EARLY CHILDHOOD MEMORIES CENTER on happenings in Denning, Texas, a farming community located between San Augustine and Nacogdoches, Texas. Granny and Papaw Worry lived there for many years, including the time when I endured my most acute growing pains, from 1949 to 1957. In this period of time, my mind and body changed from those of a child to those of a young lady. It was when I grew in wisdom and stature under the tutelage of those two special people.

Granny and Papaw lived on a red dirt road. When it rained, the red clay and mud hill leading up Manor Hill became a slick, muddy mess. On rainy Friday nights as we traveled from Pineland to Granny and Papaw's, I fretted and whined every mile worrying about how we would get up Manor Hill. Daddy never helped much either. By the time we got there, he had me convinced we would have to leave the car at the bottom of the hill and walk to Granny's house in the mud. Little boys would love that idea, but I was a persnickety little girl and did not want to get my shoes muddy.

The little white house stood among magnificent pecan trees in the midst of a big yard. I remember pulling up to the whitewashed frame house. A warm feeling of contentment enveloped me and I knew this was a house full of love for me and my family. Granny opened the door with a smile of joy when she saw me opening the rickety gate and running up the steps. The hug and kisses were filled with a peace every child should know and feel.

The Fireplace Room

The house was not large and very plain. It only had four rooms. To my small eyes it seemed much, much larger than it is as I see it from adult eyes. The living room (or fireplace room) was not lavishly furnished. Two bedsteads filled the little room, with a trail in between and a small visiting area in front of the fireplace. One of these beds was a feather bed, where Granny and Papaw slept during the wintertime to be near the fireplace. The feathers in that bed enveloped your body and wrapped you up in their warmth. The other bed was filled with cotton from the field that provided a sturdy mattress to lie on.

The only other furniture in that room was an old dresser with Granny and Papaw's Bibles stacked upon it, a corner table holding the kerosene lamp, and another corner table housing the battery-operated radio. Homemade straight-backed wooden chairs were brought from the dining table for sitting. The wooden floor was immaculately clean, as was the rest of the room. Starched cloths covered the little tables, decorated with hand-embroidered edges. The fireplace mantle held the box of matches for lighting the fire alongside Granny's snuff box and Papaw's Prince Albert tobacco and the papers for rolling his cigarettes.

Kitchen and Dining Room

A doorway opened from the fireplace room to the kitchen and dining area. The dining table was a long wooden table, with its obviously homemade rough-hewn wide planks for its top. It sported a clean, bright-colored oilcloth. Another oil lamp was situated in the middle of the table for lighting at night. Along the back wall behind the table was a long wooden bench where Papaw and I sat. On the other side of the table were straight wooden chairs with wooden slats or rope on their seat areas. There were also two of these chairs at the ends of the table. The bench could seat three if we scrunched up, so the table could seat seven or eight people. These were the only chairs I remember the house having, and were the ones brought into the fireplace room for sitting. The chair bottoms were covered with little flat cushions made of colorful calico stuffed with cotton. The colors usually did not match, but nobody cared or noticed.

Granny's stove would certainly baffle a young cook today. You see, Granny did not have electricity yet in the little house. The rural electric company finally got there about 1952. The stove was a heavy iron wood-burning piece. A large round pipe attached to the back tunneled through the roof to expel the smoke outside. The top had two or three burners, with a wood box under the burners on the left side that had to be filled and lit for the heat to cook food. The small oven was located under the burners on the right side, beside the firebox. A woman had to be quite an engineer to get the fire built just right to provide the heat she needed for the oven and for the frying pan as well. Her stove did not have any knobs to turn for "low," "medium," or "high." She had to figure it out herself, and every stove was a little different. I cannot imagine how they ever got a cake baked, cookies or biscuits made, but they did. That tiny oven could produce the most mouthwatering buttermilk biscuits, almost crawling out of the pan, or sweet potatoes with juice squeezing out of them into the pan as they baked. The iron skillet atop the stove could fry up the best pork sausage, thick-sliced bacon, or ribs you ever smacked your jaws on. I have never tasted any purple hull peas with a ham hock in them or cream-style corn that outdid that old stove and Granny's magic hands. Of course, there were the blackberry or dewberry cobblers baked in the black deep-dish aluminum pan with sugar glistening on the biscuit-top crust, swimming in homemade butter! Got your mouth watering now?

The elaborate cabinet space still amazes me. Even as a child, I wondered how Granny could find anything in that small cabinet table next to the stove. There were no overhead cabinets, only a couple of shelves to house plates, saucers, cups, glasses, and bowls. It was covered with a cotton curtain (made usually from a flour sack). Under the windows in the kitchen was a smaller table, up against the wall with all sides covered by another curtain like the one for the shelves. Under this table were no shelves or drawers, just space that Granny filled. She placed her big tin can with a lid on it in there. That big can held a fifty-pound sack of flour. She called it the "flour barrel." Pots were hung on nails or stuck underneath this table. Spoons, forks, and knives for the table were kept in a fruit jar on the dining table.

Between the stove and back door stood the food safe, where cooked foods were kept behind the screen-covered doors for protection from flies and bugs. Sometimes today this is called a "pie safe," but in East Texas before refrigeration, they were used to keep all foods "safe." The old safe has many other stories of its life, and one of them is in this book.

Bedrooms

There were two bedrooms in the little house. One was immediately off the kitchen in the back. It had lots of windows and was shaded nicely by the pecan trees in the back yard. I remember it as the cool bedroom. You will notice in my description of the kitchen that there was not a refrigerator mentioned. The only kind of cooling device they had was an icebox, which they kept in that back bedroom. The icebox was a square-shaped insulated box. They bought ice from a man who delivered it from the ice house in San Augustine. The large fifty-pound chunks were sized to fit into the ice bin at the top of the icebox. The doors were kept closed and ice could be chipped off the big chunk as needed. There was a drip pan underneath the ice and it had to be emptied regularly as the ice melted. This invention kept the butter and milk cool and that's about all.

The icebox was quite a luxury because prior to it, the only way they kept milk and butter cool in the summertime was to put it in a bucket and lower the bucket down into the water well. It was cooler underneath the ground and was the only means of preserving it for a day or so. Can you imagine living without refrigeration?

Besides the bed and the icebox in this bedroom, there was the quilt box. This was a very large box-type storage bin with a lid on it where Granny stored her large supply of quilts and linens. This big box was full to the brim and was kept clean and definitely was not to be bothered by us children. Along a wall in this room were shelves from floor to ceiling where Granny housed all her beautiful canned goods and kept her empty jars until next canning season. These shelves were usually crammed full of jellies, jams, preserves, beans, peas, potatoes, tomatoes, tomato juice, soup mixtures, cucumber pickles, beets, and chow-chow. The shelves were also neatly covered with flour-sack curtains because Granny wanted things to look nice.

During the summer months, newspapers were spread on the floor in front of the shelves and there they laid out tomatoes to ripen, and cantaloupes or watermelons.

The front bedroom was off the fireplace room at the front of the house. It had a bed and table in one corner with a lamp on it for nighttime. Another item in this room that really intrigued me was the trunk at the end of the bed. Maybe it fascinated me because I did not know what was in it, or because I was told it belonged to Papaw and I was never to bother it. I wanted to look in it so awfully bad, but I was a little bit afraid of what might happen if I did!

Granny's old treadle-type Singer sewing machine was also kept in this front bedroom. There she made dresses, curtains, sheets, and pillowcases, and patched up whatever clothing needed mending.

Between the two bedrooms was a little room that probably was built as a bathroom, but there was never one installed as long as Granny and Papaw lived there. It had shelves for storage and was packed full of goodies that were interesting to nosy hands like mine. We did take a bath in there in the washtub with water heated up in the big cistern outside that caught the rainwater. In the summer, the water was so nice and warm to take a bath. We surely needed one, because my cousins and I seemed to attract red dirt by just going out the back door. I never thought of how many steps Granny and Papaw had to take to prepare for our baths, bringing in the tub and the water and making sure all was just right for us. I do know that she would have done all she could to keep our dirty red feet and knees out of her spotlessly clean beds! And I surely do not blame her for that.

Maybe it was not a mansion. It did not have any modern gadgets like electricity, indoor plumbing, a television or telephone, but it had something money could never buy. My time at this haven was stopped on my fourteenth birthday one June night when Granny's time was up. She went to that home prepared for her many years before. At the time, I did not know what I lost. But I cherish those memories every day of my life as I get older. I had an education better than most by living at the little farmhouse on Manor Hill in the summertime. Something about that place lingers in my heart in a special way that I shall never forget.

ALL DAY SINGIN' AND DINNER ON THE GROUND

Every summer, the little Church of Christ at Lone Star (between Pineland and Brookeland, Texas) had a gospel meeting. The Baptists had "revivals" but we had "gospel meetings." I truly do not know what the difference was between a revival and a gospel meeting, except that we were different. But that was what we called them! Approximately six wooden-slat benches were placed on both sides of the "sanctuary" with a narrow aisle in the middle. Each bench would seat about five adults unless one of the larger folks was there. Then it would seat only three people. Each wall was graced with ample windows with no screens to keep out the wasps, flies, dirt daubers, and the humid heat of summer. They were raised to the top with a stick stuck under them to keep them from falling. This was the scene in the summer.

A podium stood at the front of that sanctuary with one step up so the preacher could be seen well. A chalkboard hung on the wall behind the podium for the preacher's use to draw, write, and slash arrows back and forth during his sermon. It was indeed the first PowerPoint presentation of the day.

A communion table sat on the floor level in front of the podium with the words "In Remembrance" engraved on its front. This was to remind us of the purpose of the communion service: remembering the death, burial, and resurrection of Jesus. Covering the communion table was a starched white scarf, provided by some good sister, where the communion set was laid. Sometimes someone brought fresh flowers out of their yard to adorn the table with God's natural gift of beauty. In cold weather, the windows were closed and a butane heater was placed at the front of the little room near the pulpit, making those sitting in the back row pretty chilly.

I grew up in the Church of Christ, so we had no piano or organ and most likely could not have afforded it if we wanted one. Many other churches had a piano located in the front of their little buildings. The Lone Star Church of Christ was plain and simple, a very straightforward church of the 1940s and 1950s. On a good Sunday (if we had visitors), we were delighted when more than twenty were in attendance.

On the last Sunday of a gospel meeting, usually held in June, excitement was high. There was to be a "dinner on the ground" after services that day. No, we did not eat off the ground like at a picnic, but sawhorses were brought in by some carpenter member and strategically placed under the big oak trees outside. Sawhorses were used by carpenters for building and sawing, and sometimes as a platform when working on their homes or barn. Wide boards were placed from one to the other, making a table. The women all brought tablecloths or sheets to cover the rugged, splintery tables. That was where the food would be placed.

It always seemed to me as though the preacher got longer-winded on that Sunday sermon than on other days. I guess he had no idea that no one was listening. All were thinking about that big coconut cake they knew was in Aunt Dot's car, waiting to be sliced for us to enjoy. The scent coming from the big pot of chicken dumplings sitting on the floor behind the back bench was causing stomachs to rumble. Other dishes were brought from cars and the heat into the church building and either placed on a back pew or on the floor waiting for dinnertime to come. Some of those dishes were: fried chicken, potato salad, fresh-sliced tomatoes, cream-style corn right out of the garden, fried okra, cornbread, biscuits, and banana pudding. Who could concentrate on hellfire and brimstone when heaven was waiting outside the door?

As soon as the last *Amen* was said, the women bustled about getting tables ready for their food. Husbands were instructed to bring the big cardboard boxes packed with food to the tables. We had no such thing as paper plates back in these early days, so families brought plates and silverware and such for their families, along with glasses or cups for the iced tea we would have to drink. Since there was no refrigeration there, Mr. Elmer brought a washtub with a block of ice in the back of his pickup truck from his little country store. He and Ms. Callie wrapped the tub tightly with a heavy quilt to insulate the ice so it would still be good at dinnertime. He would then chip off chunks of ice to fit into tea glasses as they were offered to him.

Kids were running around playing chase and hide-and-seek and getting sweaty and dirty every minute. The men would bring the benches outside for people to sit on while they ate lunch. Remember, there were no folding chairs then either. The men would gather up under a big tree and visit while they waited on dinner. Women would try to corral their children, who were running rampant while their fathers seemed oblivious to it all. My problem was that my dad only had me to keep up with so he kept a sharp eye out to see what I was up to. Needless to say, I tended to get in much trouble and was often called to sit down under the tree near where Daddy was visiting. I pouted but it didn't change his mind.

After a lengthy prayer before the meal, the great feast began. It got quiet out under those trees at Lone Star as our mouths became occupied with the bounty on our overloaded plates. I remember that after our lunch my mother and the other women would fill their plates and cover their food containers with lids or dish towels to keep the flies away. Only then did they get to sit down for their dinner and rest a bit. They enjoyed visiting with each other as well. They discussed recipes, quilting projects, crochet and embroidery patterns in detail. It was a really joyful time for them.

Eventually, the remaining bowls, pots, and sweets were placed back in their boxes and left to rest in the shade. That is when the songbooks were passed out for everyone to prepare to sing. It was easy for us at the Church of Christ because we didn't sing with a piano anyway so we just opened up and let 'er fly. My dad was usually one of the song leaders, and he would always lead songs that were lively. He used to say that he just didn't like those "ol' draggy songs!" His were songs like "Gloryland Way," "I'll Fly Away," "To Canaan's Land I'm On My Way," "Home of the Soul," and on and on. Other song leaders would follow with things the little old ladies liked, such as "Precious Memories," "I Want To Be a Worker For the Lord," "Higher Ground," and "Amazing Grace."

By then it would be mid-afternoon or later and the summer heat was getting unbearable as the shade moved away from tables. All was cleared, the sawhorses were put in the back of somebody's pickup truck along with the boards making up our tables, benches were put back in the church, cars were cranked, and everybody bid one another good-by with hefty hugs and handshakes.

That always reminds me of the old song that goes, "What a day that will be, when my Jesus I shall see. When I look upon His face and behold his saving grace. Then He'll take me by the hand and lead me through the Promised Land. What a day, glorious day, that will be" – and it certainly was. And it surely will be.

BOB WHITE

Written September 7 (year unknown)
By Richmond Pierce Veatch

The meadows are shining with golden grain
The yellow leaves are falling.
And I hear in the autumn twilight
A bobwhite gently calling.

He hears his neighbor voices
While the early dew is falling
And along the hazy upland wide
I hear him softly calling.

The sky is darkening overhead
Without a sign of warning
And I hear him in the meadow
Gently calling, calling, calling.

CALLIE AND ELMER

They were old. At least, to me they seemed old. She had light brown hair with tinges of gray. His was dark brown, slicked straight back from his forehead with some kind of hair oil to make it lie in place. They owned a country store with lots of goodies in it that made my six-year-old mouth water. My parents were their friends and we visited them quite often.

They lived in the back of the store but I was never allowed back there. When we went to visit, we sat in chairs and on the bench at the front of the store. Their names were Callie and Elmer. I loved to visit them because they had no children and thought I was just about the cutest thing in Brookeland, Texas. I loved being center stage and, as an only child, thought that was the way life should be run. I served as the entertainment, front and center. But Callie and Elmer taught me some life lessons they never knew they were teaching.

My parents averaged visiting their friends at least once a week. Daddy and Elmer would drink coffee and discuss things at the sawmill where my daddy worked. They also discussed the world situation and politics. Mama and Callie talked about crochet patterns and new material they had for sewing or quilting. I bounced from one place to another, being constantly reminded not to touch things. Since they had no children, it seemed to me that I must be a blessing to them by showing how wonderful it would be to have a little girl who was curious about every little thing and asked questions one after another. Callie seemed to enjoy me but Elmer hardly ever paid me any attention, much to my dismay.

Christmastime was a wonderful time to visit them because Callie made the best candy you ever ate. She made fudge and beautiful, perfect divinity. Mother would only allow me a piece of each but if I was sneaky, Callie would give me another to take home with me. Needless to say, it never made it past the back seat of the old Dodge coupe we drove at the time.

I have thought a lot about why I so vividly remember Callie and Elmer besides just the friendship with my parents and the fact that Callie was a faithful member of the church we attended. Elmer never came to church but he was always there to pick Callie up after services and visit with all who attended. There were no toys at their place. I was not allowed to touch things in the store. I was never allowed to the back of the store where they lived. It sounds like it would be a really boring place for a child to go, yet I remember it and them so vividly.

One night after we left their store to go home, the headlights on our old Dodge went out. It was black as could be out in the flat, wooded area of the Brookeland bottom (now covered by waters from Sam Rayburn Dam). Daddy pulled to the side of the road and took the flashlight he always carried with him to see if he could fix the lights. All I could see and hear was blackness and the frogs loudly proclaiming the night with their songs. Crickets chirped in their rhythm, but not another sound was heard. There was not much night traffic in those days and that night there was none. Daddy came back to the window and told Mama that he needed bulbs for the lights and of course had none with him. He could not see how to safely drive home.

That's when I tuned up to cry in the back seat because I was scared. If my daddy could not fix it, we were in big trouble, I thought. He told

Mama he was going to walk back to Elmer's and get him to come drive ahead of us home and Mama and I just needed to stay in the car. I was sniveling and crying and doing all the things a little kid does when they are afraid. Mama was not afraid of anyone bothering us because back in those days, a person who came along would have stopped to try to help, not harm. So we played a game to see how many sounds we could identify and in no time Mama saw the headlights of a car coming. It was Elmer and Daddy in Elmer's old truck. He got ahead of our car and told Daddy to drive right behind him so he could see the way home. We got home safe and sound thanks to a friend.

That night I learned about friends helping one another. No money exchanged hands. Elmer got up from his comfortable home to come out at night for about an hour and see us home safely. He taught me a lot about friendship that night.

It finally came to me that I learned a lot from these visits. I was taught how to act when visiting in another person's home that was not family. I must show respect for things belonging to other people. I was to listen when adults were speaking and to act according to directions. If I did not, my daddy's look or tone of voice would stop me in my tracks. I heard how adults spoke to one another about world affairs, things that interested them and were important in an adult world. I got attention but I was not the center of attention all the time. I learned how to act as a guest. I learned about friendship.

Children in today's world do not have a clue about the above things, for the most part not because their parents are so busy working and trying to survive but because they rarely visit anyone other than family. Just going out to eat with children today is an ordeal of temper fits, disobedience, and lack of respect for the property of others and for the food they waste. It seems like such a simple lesson to learn but it must be taught. The lesson of good friends is one that is most valuable today. Good friends and unselfish friendship is hard to find in the world today.

These are the things I learned from my visits to Callie and Elmer's store. Respect, listening skills, the value of good friends, following directions, and not being the center of attention are important lessons. Why are they so hard to teach today? They are not – we just do not make the time.

CECIL'S STORY

He was not alone in the womb. His twin brother shared it with him, but although they were born on the same day, September 1, 1915, their similarities were few from that point forward. Being born in 1915 in a small unpainted wood frame house on the banks of McKim Creek in Sabine County, Texas, gave them a difficult start to begin with. Their father, Sam Veatch, was a farmer, and they were numbers eight and nine of the total clan. Sam was getting old and tired by then. Nan, their mother, stood at less than five feet tall and had borne all these children, fed and clothed them the best she could, and she was weary of children. So Cecil and his brother, Murry, were left pretty much to their own devices as they grew.

Cecil and Murry were a pair, and kept the rest of the family busy just trying to keep up with them. Their parents gave them strict orders as little boys to stay away from the creek. They were three or four years old when they could not be found one day and their father, Sam, started toward the creek to look for them. He heard them before he saw them. They were playing near the creek, totally oblivious to everything and everyone. Sam stopped and hid behind a big log just to watch them for a bit, probably enjoying the antics of his two youngest children and relieved that they were safe. The boys must have heard the leaves rustle when he lay down behind the log because one of them said, "What was that?"

To which the other one replied, "I don't know but let's go see!" Not afraid of anything or anybody in those woods, they stumbled upon their daddy watching over them. He brought them back to the house, probably with some sage words of advice. But I'm almost positive they went back as soon as they had a chance.

But back to Cecil's story. Cecil was a little blond-haired kid, skinny and mischievous. Their oldest sister, Hattie, was given the job of trying to keep them alive and take care of them as best she could. So she witnessed many of Cecil's tricks and troublesome activities as he grew. As they grew into men, we found that both these little boys seemed to gravitate to Hattie's house and to visit often with her. After all, she was their sister/mother!

The family has all heard stories of our ancestor, Dr. John Allen Veatch, whose wanderlust led him to the Mexican War for Texas Independence, and from there to California as part of the Gold Rush. He could not seem to stay still in one place very long, and as I look over Cecil's life, I see some of that same characteristic in him.

He worked for the WPA in several parts of East Texas while they built roads and began the early infrastructure of our part of the world. His first love that lasted him all his life was music. He very early on managed to teach himself how to play the guitar. He moved on from there to the banjo, a little on the fiddle and the mandolin, and I'm not sure exactly what other instruments he could play. He had no formal training, just an inborn natural talent of "hearing" music and being able to play a song upon hearing the music on the radio. He developed his playing to include songwriting and singing. Little country bands of folks loving music would entertain on Saturday nights at someone's house with audiences of friends and neighbors. Many of these people had organs or pianos; add to that the music of the country boys with guitars, fiddles, harmonicas, and banjos and quite a party developed. There were barn dances in neighborhoods and Cecil and his rag-tag band would manage to find a way there to play and sing.

Along with the dances and parties was always a little "hooch" somewhere outside to be enjoyed. In case you don't know, hooch was a slang word for alcoholic beverages, usually home brewed in a still somewhere deep in the woods and served up in fruit jars. It was potent and could make one feel really happy as they got inebriated – or it might make a few of them ready to fight. You could never tell. Cecil got happy. He could play all night long and never miss a beat if he had a little hooch on the side. Of course, this totally went against the teaching and beliefs of his father and mother, but as he grew into a young man, he took things into his own hands and went his way.

After he'd bounced around from one job to another, one place to another, the Big War loomed on the horizon. Not one to shirk his duty to his country, Cecil enlisted. He served out his first term before the war got really in the thick of things. He got out of the service when things were getting worse overseas and, undaunted, he re-enlisted. As one of his letters back home stated, "I'm fixin' to go on a really long boat ride." He was about to go overseas.

We know from letters he sent to his twin brother that he was in Germany, Belgium, and Sicily, and most would say, "Somewhere in Belgium" or wherever when he sent them home. Things back in Brookeland, Texas, went on pretty much as usual. Three of the Veatch boys were serving in the military during the war. John was in England, Virgil was in Belgium and France, and Cecil was all over the place. Murry escaped serving because he was employed by Temple Lumber Company in Pineland, Texas, and they had contracts to build bomb crates and other materials for the war. He served by working for them during the war and was the one left at home to take care of his widowed mother. Sam had died in 1930 of a massive stroke so Nan was living with one child or another during this period. Murry took care of a lot of her business and physical needs during this time while the brothers were gone.

Cecil served as a medical aide during the World War II era. He was trained at Breckenridge Hospital in San Antonio before he shipped out. I often have wondered if he volunteered to be a medical aide or if somehow they drafted him to fill that position. He had no medical experience but also no fear of anything. Maybe the Army saw that in that young blond-haired boy from East Texas and decided he was what they needed to go into the thick of things. He always wrote about somebody sending him guitar strings, so even in a war zone, he was playing music, writing songs, and making people laugh. He loved to make people laugh and play jokes on whomever he could. His name given him by his fellow soldiers was Tex. That is how he signed his letters during those days, and the nickname stuck for many years afterward. Tex faced the enemy, he faced the injured, and he brought back the dead from the battlefield. He signed a story he wrote about a battle he endured by saying that he fought in five major battles with General George S. Patton during WWII. I don't know which major battles they were and I so wish I did. I watched the documentary-drama miniseries *Band of Brothers*, and as the medics were called for often on the battlefield, my imagination could see my uncle Cecil there. His face was grim, bullets and bombs whizzing by him while he was focused on that soldier who depended on him to get him to safety. I could see him pulling back those he knew were not going to make it, taking their last words and promising to get them back to their loved ones if he could. At night around their blacked-out camp, he strummed on his guitar, looked at the stars under the German night sky, and thought about home. Then he found something to dim the faces, to stop the pain, and he drank.

He lived through those awful war-filled days, those days that smelled of death and decay, and he came back home to Brookeland, Texas, in 1946, but he was not the same boy who'd left. He was a man who hid his hurt, destroyed his pain as he destroyed himself, with alcohol. He got jobs in which he was a good employee. But when Friday evening came, paycheck in hand, he was picked up from work by those who claimed to be his buddies and the numbing of his senses began.

He went to Detroit, Michigan, and worked for a time for Ford Motor Company in their plant there. He made good money and occasionally sent some home to his mother. The family heard little from him during this period and his twin was worried. He knew somehow that something bad was wrong with Cecil. But none of them knew how to contact him. One day, word came back to his older brother, John, that Cecil was in bad trouble in Detroit. The family heard nothing and Detroit was too far away for anyone to go check on him. They all just worried.

After a time, he returned to Texas and worked on the farm for his sister Hattie's husband and lived with them. He eventually went to work for Visador Company of Jasper, Texas, in the millwork area for several years. He was a good employee but he drank. It was his crutch and it was the way he dealt with his life. He lived during this period of time with his sister, Viola, in Jasper. He built bird boxes, windmills, bookshelves, and other decorative items with wood in his little shop out of her house. He sold some, he gave away more. He was about to lose his job at Visador because of his drinking and he knew it. He just couldn't stop.

So one day he told his sister that on that next Friday evening, he was going to California with a friend of his. He would let her know how he was doing every now and then. He left and again the family knew nothing of his whereabouts or his life situation. He was now in his fifties and had treated his body with total disregard for years. It would take its toll.

One day in early June, 1970, his brother John received a call from Cecil's friend, who had been taking care of him for some time, saying that Cecil had died in the V.A. Hospital in San Fernando, California, on June 11, 1970. He was fifty-four years, nine months, and ten days old. Murry and John wanted to bring him back home to Texas for burial so they put up what money they could gather, with help from Hattie and Viola, and John flew to Los Angeles, California, to bring his brother back home.

His funeral was held in Jasper at Stringer Funeral Home and the remaining family was there: John, Murry, Viola, Ollie, Hattie, and Virgil all sadly watched and bade their brother goodbye. There was a military funeral and the folded American flag was given to his twin brother. He did not die in World War II, but he did give his life there. He tried to go on but he could not wash away the pain, the faces, the death and destruction he saw as a medical aide there. He was buried in Memorial Park Cemetery in Jasper, Texas, with a military funeral and marker at his grave.

Years later when his twin brother was in his eighties, he decided he wanted a better marker at the head of the grave of his brother. He bought a single marker that stands at the head of his grave and the military flat marker now lies at his feet. It was such a terrible loss of such a talented man. One who gave his life for this country, so much so that he could not live after he came home. He lies there today three graves down from his mother, whom he loved so much. I try to mark it with flowers and flag on the appropriate days. He should be honored.

Thank you, Corporal Cecil F. Veatch, for your service as a medical aide in World War II under General George S. Patton.

CHORES AND DAY'S END

A LOT OF WORK HAS to be done on a farm, and my grandparents' farm on Manor Hill was no exception. When I was there, I was expected to help with a few things. The farm had a few milk cows, chickens, and hogs. There were a couple of horses to pull Papaw's plow in the fields he farmed. All these animals had to be cared for in the morning and evening.

Granny and Papaw arose early in the morning and went to milk the cows. Granny came back to the house to take care of the milk. She believed in everything being clean and done right so this was her job. Papaw went back to the barn and slopped the hogs and made sure they hadn't broken a board on the fence in an attempt to escape. He released the cows from the cow lot and they headed out into the pasture to graze all day and make more milk. The horses had to be fed as well before they were put out in the pasture, unless he was going to use them to plow that day. If so, they were left in the enclosure of a small pasture until he was ready to hook up the plow.

Before Granny got through straining the milk, she started a fire in the stove and made a pan of biscuits for breakfast. When the stove got hot, in would go the biscuit pan. Then she sliced off some pieces of ham from the smokehouse or some bacon and let it sizzle in the iron skillet on top of the stove. She boiled the coffee on the top of the stove in the coffee pot as well. While breakfast cooked, she strained the milk.

I was not awake during the early chores but the smell of biscuits and bacon, sausage, or ham got my attention and I was ready to go. We made quick work of those biscuits and homemade fig preserves. In late evening, the chores were repeated. There is a time that still comes to me many evenings as the day comes to an end. I remember it as being the "golden time" of the day. The sun sunk low enough that it shone into the fireplace room windows, creating a golden aura in the house. I knew it was time to do chores again. Granny fed the chickens and gathered the eggs. I helped gather the eggs a few times, but mostly I just followed her around, watching, learning, and being close to her.

Papaw fed the horses and slopped the hogs again. I did not do anything much with the horses because they were so big and I was a little afraid of them. But I loved to watch the hogs eat. They were so awfully dirty (about the only thing that could get dirtier than I could) and stunk so badly.

Granny and Papaw went back to the house with the milk buckets filled with fresh warm milk straight from old Jersey's bag. The milk we were going to drink was strained and put into the icebox to keep cool or, in winter, just left sitting in the safe because the house would be as cold as outside was. The other milk was put into containers to sour and later be churned to make butter and buttermilk. There was also clabbered milk that Papaw loved to drink. It had chunks of soured milk and he mixed it up, put a little sugar in it, stirred it up, and told me it was good. I refused to try his concoction. You do know what yogurt is, don't you?

When chores were over it was nearly dark and stillness settled over the little farm. One could tell that night and resting time was approaching. Supper was served in the kitchen at the big table and was usually leftover things from lunch. In summertime we had our baths and settled down on the front porch, where I watched and chased fireflies and listened to the whippoorwills deep down in the woods calling to one another. Granny and Papaw talked about a lot of things. I was running about but listening and learning. In wintertime we gathered around the fireplace, where Papaw rolled his Prince Albert tobacco into cigarettes and Granny mended shirts and socks or worked on piecing a quilt top by hand until it was too difficult to see by lamplight. That was when she stopped. By then my head was nodding onto my chest and I was ready to get to my bed for the night.

Saturday nights were the exception to the rule. That was the night the old battery radio was tuned up loud and clear to WSM in Nashville, Tennessee, for the Saturday night Grand Ole Opry. We heard Little Jimmy Dickens, Grandpa Jones, Roy Acuff, and Faron Young singing country hits of the day. Minnie Pearl and Rod Brasfield were performing their comedy routines. The kitchen was cleaned up, baths were taken, and we gathered in our chairs to listen to the program. It was the week's entertainment. In the wintertime, the fire was roaring and snapping and our front sides were warm while our backsides were chilled. But nobody there minded because it was the best you'd ever had. It was also a time you never forgot. That is the way it was.

COUNTRY CHURCHES

Going to church was a lot like going to a family reunion. Of course, church *should* be like that all the time…but it was more so in the late 1940s and '50s. There were not many folks there when we had a "good" crowd. Although there were several kinds of churches in the area where my grandparents lived, the one I am going to tell you about is the Ratcliff Church of Christ, located between San Augustine and Nacogdoches, Texas. There were Baptist, Methodist, and Pentecostal churches in the area but the small rural Church of Christ was where we went.

The white wooden-frame building, located about three miles from Granny and Papaw's house, was rectangular shaped with a room built onto the side for a classroom and one onto the back for classrooms. The adults met in the auditorium area of the building while children met in the classrooms. The auditorium probably had a seating capacity of about fifty and wooden benches filled the space. Floors were wooden, as well as walls and pews, thus if you dropped a songbook, it was *loud!* Cooling in the summer was raised windows (no screens) and open doors. There were ceiling fans that helped some. Songbooks were the old blue ones in wooden racks made of narrow slats on the backs of the pews. They bumped loudly when being removed or placed back in the racks.

Oh, but the singing! It bounced off those wooden walls and floor and certainly was from the heart. Very few people, if any, knew one note from another and it really didn't matter. The songs were written in the songbooks in what is called "shaped notes," and people had been taught to sing by learning the Do-Re-Mi method. There were "singing schools" conducted at times to teach people the shaped notes and how to read music that way. However, most just sang and tried to follow the leader. When we were visiting there, my dad was asked to lead singing. The same songs were usually sung each time and most knew them from memory. Sometimes it seems to me that's why they sang so much from their hearts – they did not need a book to tell them what to sing. These people who had no music training except what they learned from home sang parts quite well. We had good bass and tenor, and those old ladies could come down on that alto! We had no piano or musical instruments and "singing" is what we did.

The Ratcliff Church of Christ met on Sunday afternoon at two o'clock. The reason for that was they were so small they could not pay a preacher full time, so the preacher from San Augustine came out in the afternoon and preached for the little church. Then he went back to San Augustine to preach that night. Not many preachers today would think of preaching three times on the Lord's Day. He was a very busy man.

One preacher during the time I attended there as a child was Brother Kreager. He was probably in his mid-fifties and quite a colorful fellow. He preached on a level children could understand, with lots of emotion and action. I loved it! Another thing he did was come by and pick us up for church and bring us home. You see, Papaw and Granny had no means of transportation except the wagon. So the good preacher came by to take them to church almost every Sunday. And either he or a member of the San Augustine church came by every night of a gospel meeting so Granny and Papaw could attend.

Bible class there was different from those of today. In the younger children's class, with several ages in the same room, the teacher started out by holding her Bible in her lap and telling us the story for that day. A good teacher could hold our attention with no problem, especially if she was a good storyteller.

The class for older children probably started with fifth grade and went through high school. They studied straight out of the Bible. It is a wonder we learned anything from the teaching tools used, but we got the basics in those classes. They have stayed with most of us all of our lives.

The other country church we attended was Lone Star Church of Christ, located in Brookeland, Texas, now near the backwaters of Lake Sam Rayburn Dam. I was very small when we went to Lone Star church, but it was my home congregation that I remember as a child. It was a lot the same as the Ratcliff Church I just described, but their building was even smaller. It was a tiny building of wood with wooden benches made of slats on the seats and back. Those slats were an excellent way to pinch little legs or get a splinter when wiggling too much. Yes, I know that from experience!

One thing that I feel we had back then that we sometimes miss now is that we were all a "family." Attendance was pretty regular because it was the highlight of everyone's week. There was nothing interfering with going to church in those days because there were no other activities pulling us away from worship like there are today. Everyone knew everyone else and their whole family, and if anything was wrong in our life you could count on our church family being there for us. These folks were busy in many ways also. They were busy trying to survive with little money and hard work. Many churches today work hard to find this family atmosphere, but Satan has put so many things before us to pull us away that it is hard to keep us close.

Have we lost sight of something very important now? What we did not have in numbers, we had in faithfulness. That is the way it was.

DADDY BUILT A HOUSE

The tiny two-bedroom shack of a house that we'd moved into when Daddy bought the place at Holly Springs became too crowded when my granny passed away. My grandfather chose to come live with us because he needed help in the last years of his life. I had to give up my tiny bedroom to him. I was fourteen years old. No, I did not throw a tantrum and demand something better. The thought never occurred to me, but if it had, my daddy would have quickly rectified that situation. So my bed was squeezed into the same room as Mama and Daddy's.

One spring I noticed there were drawings of house plans lying about on the dining table, lots of figuring going on and stops made at the local building-supply place. One day, Daddy said he was going to talk to a man at the bank about borrowing some money. Kids were supposed to be seen, not heard in those days of the mid-1950s, so I just waited around and watched to see what would happen next.

Daddy came back to the house with a big grin on his face one day and I heard him telling Mama he got the money. I just wandered into the kitchen, where they were, and Daddy told me to sit down with him and Mama at the table. He pulled out one of those big sheets of paper with the lines drawn on them and said, "I'm going to build us a new house."

I was excited and not sure I understood what that meant. He told me he had talked with his cousin, Elmer, and he was going to help him. Work would start on the foundation the next Saturday. He said it would take a while because they both had jobs and they could only work on the house after work and on Saturdays and holidays off.

I asked, "Where is it going to be?"

Daddy said it would be right behind our little house, and that when the new house was finished he would tear down the old one. I would have my own bedroom, Papaw would have his bedroom, and Mama and Daddy would have theirs. The big news, he said, was that we would have an indoor bathroom and toilet.

He built two big rooms onto the back of our little house first, which we entered through a door from the kitchen. They would be my bedroom and Mama and Daddy's bedroom. Shortly after we finished those rooms and moved into them, my papaw Worry passed away. The building stopped for a good while. We grieved for him and it takes time to heal.

Eventually, Daddy and Elmer started adding a really big foundation to the back of our bedrooms. That foundation was not concrete, but was to be built on piers and beams out of wood. The plan was that the two bedrooms we already had would become a living room and a kitchen/dining room when the new part was finished. The new part was three big bedrooms and a bathroom. It took a long time.

As a matter of fact, the new part got finished, the old house was torn away, and a front porch was built by October 1966 when I got married. Our wedding reception was held at this house. Daddy built the kitchen cabinets himself and they were beautiful. He and Elmer did everything but the electrical wiring; a good friend came and did that for them.

This was the house I brought my babies to after they were born. This was the house where Nannie and Papaw kept them while I worked for many years until they started school. This was the house they rode the school bus to, and where they walked up the same dirt road I had after school. This was the house we built our home next door to in 1977. This was the house that stood through a tornado tearing through the woods directly in front of it. This was the house where I saw my mama's and daddy's health decline until their deaths.

And this was the house that Hurricane Rita damaged so badly I had to have it torn on down because I couldn't stand to look at it in that shape. It was special to my heart and still is today. When it stood there empty, falling down, water pouring inside because of the roofing being rolled up like paper, looking at it hurt my heart. I kept waiting for Mama to come out with her bonnet on to work on her flowers. I could see Daddy sitting on the screened back porch with a jaw full of chewing tobacco looking out at his garden. It was time for the house to go.

Daddy used to say, "Well, this ol' house will last me as long as I need one. I guess that's long enough." He was right.

DID SHE OR DIDN'T SHE?

The four first cousins had not been together in many years, except for family funerals. Here we sat, giggling about old times and old memories. Robbie was the oldest, then Faye, then Jean, then me. As the youngest in the crowd, I had questions about my paternal grandmother. There were many things I did not remember about her while I was growing up, so I started this conversation.

"Tell me about Grandma," I said. "What was she like?"

"Well, she was kind of quiet," Robbie responded.

"All I remember about her is that she walked with a limp, sat in a rocking chair, and dipped snuff," I said. "And she always gave me all her pennies."

Faye chimed in, "That's pretty much all she did all right, was sit and rock. Why did she give you her pennies?"

"She said those ol' pennies weren't worth anything to her so I could have 'em all. Back in the 1950s, if I got a few pennies to go to town with I could buy a Coke and some candy," I remembered.

Jean, who was sitting over to the side of the table and had not said a word, finally spoke. She said, "Grandma didn't wear any step-ins."

I was a little puzzled, so I asked, "Step-ins? You mean like underwear?"

"Yeah, she didn't wear any, did she, Robbie?" She looked at her sister.

That stopped us cold. Everyone looked at Jean like we hadn't heard what she said. Robbie finally said, "No, I don't think she did. At least we never saw any in the wash when we washed clothes."

This was not particularly the kind of vision I wanted to have of my grandmother, and the pictures going through my mind were just not good. That's when Faye spoke up, grinning sheepishly, and said, "I tried to find out if she did one time."

This was just getting deeper and deeper, but I plunged in anyway. "And how did you do that?" I inquired.

"Well, one time when Grandma was staying at our house, I lay down in the doorway to the room where she slept, because I knew she'd go take a nap in the afternoon. The plan was that I would lie there until she came by and check it out from the floor angle to see if she had on any underwear."

By then, all three of us were leaning over the table looking anxiously at her, secretly admiring her bravery to check out Grandma's drawers.

"Well, what did you find out?" we all asked at once.

"Didn't find out a thing. She walked by and I tried as hard as I could but she had on that ol' long apron and I couldn't see a cotton-pickin' thing!"

We all burst into hysterical laughter as we visualized the scene just described.

Faye continued, "I tried several more times until Mama threatened to spank me if I didn't quit lying on the floor in the way. I even watched her when she crossed her legs, thinking surely I could tell. No luck," she giggled.

Back then, Grandma always wore dresses down almost to her ankles and covered her legs completely. It was the proper dress for older ladies of the 1960s. We continued to discuss her, revealing that she much preferred the outside to the inside of the house. She hated housework and did very little of it. We decided if we had had nine kids in rapid succession, we probably would run outside too.

But back to the underwear dilemma: we concluded that the underwear truth about Grandma would remain a mystery. No underwear in the wash for certain, but we all knew she could rock and spit into the fireplace with absolute accuracy. But the other business we will never know for sure. And that was our memory of Grandma.

FORGOTTEN TERMS

There are many terms and sayings that are gone from our speech today that were prevalent when we were growing up. It is kind of fun to look at these and remember them, and to explain them to those reading this who don't have a clue what we are talking about. I am sure I've forgotten many, but here are some you might remember.

- **Busy as a bee in a tar bucket** – That is really, really busy.
- **Cow lot** – If you've ever been in one, you will remember that watching where you stepped was really important. It was where the cows were fed and watered and sometimes milked. In the summer, it had a very pungent odor!
- **Clothesline and clothespin sack** – After a long morning of washing clothes and scrubbing them clean on the rub-board, the next chore was to get the clothespin sack (making sure there weren't any wasps inside) and head to the clothesline to hang out the clean wash. Clothespins were wooden back in the days of the 1940s and '50s, and Mama kept hers in a homemade sack that could be hooked over your shoulder so the pins were in handy reach, or sometimes she sewed a sack that fit onto a clothes hanger and could be hooked to the clothesline as you worked. According to my mama, there was an art to hanging out clothes.

They were not to be hung just any old way – only in Ola's way! Overalls all together, work shirts together, towels together, and so on. Nothing must touch the ground and there must be ample pins on them to keep them hanging up in the breeze all day. Usually the clothesline had a board propped in the middle to lift the line up higher, as the wet clothes weighed it down once they were hung. One must pay attention!

- **Churning** – When you were churning the milk up and down with the dasher of the churn, you were about to make butter! The milk churned into buttermilk and the butter would rise to the top. It could then be skimmed off the top and worked with gentle hands to squeeze out all the liquid so only the yellow butter was left. Granny put a little salt in her butter and patted it firmly into a butter mold for shaping. She had a wooden butter mold as well as a glass one. There was a pretty little design on the top side to impress in the butter so that when it became firm, the design would show up on your slab of butter.
- **Get shut of it** – One of my dad's phrases, used when he wanted to throw something away, give it away, or just plain get rid of it. He was going to "get shut of" it.
- **I'll hope you** – I heard my grandpa Worry say that many times when I was very young and I didn't understand what he meant. He was saying, "I'll help you."
- **Sweep the yard** - If you were given this chore, it meant you got a brush broom (usually homemade) meant to be used to literally sweep the yard. Most yards were kept with no grass in them because they had no such thing as a lawn mower. The only thing to keep the yard clean of grass was a hoe or a weed-sling, used to cut grass by hand. Granny had a homemade brush broom made from corn stalks tied together and it was used to keep the yard

swept clean of leaves and litter.

- **Draw a bucket of water** – There was no running water, nor a sink in the houses, in those days. The well was generally near the back porch and one could quickly lower the well bucket down on a rope tied to its bail. It unwound down into the well from a pulley. When it reached the water level in the well, it tipped over, filling up, and then you could pull on the pulley rope and bring it up to the top for use. Well water was very cool when it came up out of the well, and getting the dipper for a long drink in the hot summertime was a treat.
- **Dipper** – The dipper hung on a nail driven in a post out on the back porch next to the shelf holding the water bucket with well water. Everybody – I mean everybody – who was thirsty grabbed that dipper, filled it with water from the bucket, and drank thirstily from it. The dipper was sometimes made from a gourd grown in the field, or it might be aluminum. Today it would be considered very unsanitary to drink from a dipper, but we did it all the time and were healthy as could be.
- **Washtub** – It was an aluminum tub that was used for many things on the farm. It was round and about a foot and a half deep. Adults could sit in it to take a bath if they scrunched their legs up some. Children fit fine and were required to scrub themselves with a "washrag" and soap. Sometimes they got sent back for a second round if it did not meet with Mama's or Granny's approval. It was also used to do laundry. It held rinse water; clothes were moved around in it and wrung out by hand.
- **Washrag** - We were pretty poor so we didn't have store-bought anything. Washrags were made from towels that were too thin to dry off with or were raveled out. They were cut into pieces and made into "washrags."

- **Slop the hogs** – In most farm homes, there was a bucket kept near the kitchen, usually in a side room, holding table scraps and used dishwater. This was used to feed the hogs when it became full enough. The farmer would pour the "slop" (as it was called) into the hot trough for the hungry hogs and pigs to eat. As soon as they heard him coming with the bucket, here the hogs came, grunting loudly and moving pretty fast for big fat animals, diving their snouts into that "slop."
- **Get up with the chickens** – All farms that had chickens always had an older, feisty rooster to rule the chicken yard where they all lived. Part of this old rooster's job, besides prancing around and bossing the hens, was to wake up the farm with his loud crowing. At the first sign of daylight, he would start rearing back and bellowing his loud crow. Now if you had some little younger roosters on the yard, they tried their best to mimic him. Their crows were high-pitched, rather thin-sounding attempts. Kind of like a young boy reaching adulthood but thinking he was as big as his daddy! Adults were usually up before the rooster crowed but he made sure all on the farm knew daylight was coming.
- **Digging taters** – Potatoes did not appear in a grocery store for us farm-raised kids. No, they grew under those nice green tops on the ground and one had to dig them out of the earth. When it was time to "dig taters," my dad would plow the row to make the potatoes roll out of the ground. My job was to get on my hands and knees and pick up the potatoes and put them in the bucket with me. It was a dirty job, and backbreaking as well, but they were sure good when Mama got them cooked for dinner.
- **Shucking corn** – Another chore, when the corn was gathered off the stalks in the garden and brought to the back yard in a bucket to be prepared for cooking or canning. Everyone started

grabbing corn and pulling the shuck (outside covering) off. I did pretty well at that until I ran into the first green worm, and then I was through! After the shuck was off, the corn silks had to be carefully removed, then sent to the kitchen.

- **Foot-tub** – I don't know where this "pail" got its name except that it was also commonly used to wash feet. Baths weren't available in a big tub every night, due to lack of water in most homes, but feet had to be washed every night. This was the tub that was used with a little water and a lot of scrubbing to wash those dirty feet – so it was a foot-tub!

I'm sure you will be able to think of many others not mentioned here. It is remarkable how our language and terms have changed over a short period of time, but it is such fun to remember.

GRANNY'S OLD SAFE

The old food safe was part of the furniture in my grandmother's kitchen. It stood about six feet tall, with two screened doors hiding two shelves at the top half of the piece and a narrow drawer dividing the middle. Two solid wooden doors closed to store items in the bottom. Its original varnish had long faded before my memory, but that was not what mattered to me. My focus upon arrival at Granny's, after the hugs and kisses, was to head for the old food safe. It always held a platter of teacakes covered with a white dish towel embroidered on either end with colorful flowers. But the real treat on that plate was a ball of raw cookie dough wrapped and saved just for me. I could hardly wait to get it.

Back in the early days of the 1950s, my grandparents lived on a red dirt road in rural East Texas. They had no electricity until the mid-1950s, and the food safe was there to protect the cooked food from flies and bugs that flew about through open windows in the summer. Its wooden shelves might contain a bowl of purple hull peas covered by a plate of leftover breakfast biscuits. Sometimes it held a bowl of yellow squash, cream-style corn, or other vegetables that had been cooked earlier in the day. But my focus was the plate on the top shelf holding the teacakes and that roll of raw cookie dough.

As I anxiously dragged a chair from the wooden dining table over in front of the safe, climbed up, and opened the screened upper portion to reveal my treat, I never noticed that the shelves were lined with brightly colored pieces of material that had originally covered a sack of flour. Nor did I notice that the screen covering the upper doors was loose on one side and the bottom two doors had to be jiggled to make them close properly. It was not a beautiful piece of elegant furniture, but it was sturdy and strong, serving its purpose.

Then I waited while Granny poured me a glass of cool milk she drew up from the bucket keeping the milk jug cool down in the well. They did not always have ice readily available, so milk and butter could be kept cool in the summertime by placing them in the bucket normally used to draw up well water. It was carefully eased down into the cool dampness of the well on its tightly knotted rope to keep milk and butter preserved in the hot summer days.

I unwrapped the soft cookie dough and smelled its strong vanilla fragrance while my mouth watered in anticipation of the flavors to come. It did not disappoint as I slowly filled my mouth with the sugary vanilla smoothness of Granny's teacake dough. These were made with eggs gathered from the nests out in the henhouse, milk that came from the Jersey cow now grazing in the pasture, butter made from that milk, and vanilla flavoring bought from the traveling Watkins salesman. If you have ever had a homemade teacake, your mouth is watering too in remembrance.

The old food safe was moved from Granny's kitchen after she died to my mother's house. It held goodies there as well, but was mostly used to house pretty dishes and bowls because we now had refrigeration and electricity. Then one day it needed a new home, because my mother's house was now empty. The old food safe was brought to my kitchen, where it holds an honored place. I do not need it to protect my food from outside insects, but I do need it to hold mementos of that past.

There are the dishes that came from Granny's kitchen, a bonnet of my mother's, and her apron. They are displayed there for all who wish to look, with stories to tell if they could but talk. Sometimes I stand and look at them wondering what they could tell me if I could hear them.

The old safe is well over one hundred years old by now and is as strong and sturdy as ever. The screen on its doors is a little loose at the top but still protects its contents. In the bottom, behind the doors that open out, Granny and Mama kept the biscuit pan. This was the pan that held the flour used to create a "flour bowl." All the ingredients for the biscuits were placed in the flour bowl and buttermilk was added until the dough was just the right consistency to become a ball. Then they pinched off a chunk of the dough, rolled it around in their hands to smooth it, and placed it in a greased pan ready for the oven. After cooking in the old wood stove or a modern gas or electric oven, the big, fluffy biscuits would almost crawl out of the pan.

Today those doors can be opened and the "flour pan" is still there in its spot. No, it does not have flour in it and has not been used to make a biscuit in many years now. But I can open the doors and see my grandmother or my mother's hands as they made ready to provide a pan of hot biscuits for breakfast in days gone by.

Yes, it is just an old piece of furniture. It could be replaced by an expensive modern hutch with etched-glass doors and shelves that are not warped. But what would I do with those memories that belong in the old safe? I don't know and I'm not ever going to find out.

HOG-KILLING DAY

It always happened when the weather was its coldest and predicted to remain so for at least three days. The temperature had to be freezing at night and not much warmer during the day in order to perform this job. It started with preparations the day before. The kitchen must be readied for a deluge of activity and the use of many big pots and pans. It needed the meat grinder attached to the end of the wooden dining table, lots of wood for the wood stove, and lots of dish-washing soap ready. It would begin as early in the morning as daylight allowed. It was hog-killing day.

In the early morning of hog-killing day, the black wash-pot was filled with water and a roaring fire was built under it. My dad and my grandfather would go out with the shotgun and coax the delegated hog (or hogs) up as near as they could get to the wash-pot by holding a bucket of food in front of it. When the perfect angle was achieved, the shot was fired in just the right spot of the jugular to drop the hog with one shot. It was important to get the animal as close to the wash-pot as possible because a fat dead hog is hard to drag any distance.

At that point, when the water in the pot was hot, the hog was placed on wooden slats, a sheet of tin, or in a leaning barrel where the water could be poured on it. This was to loosen the hog's hair for scraping him. The water could not be too hot or it would set the hair and it would remain firm. I heard of one incident when the hog killing was planned on the morning a blue norther was scheduled to arrive. About the time the hog was ready to scrape, water poured on him to loosen the hair, the norther arrived with such a vengeance and rapid lowering of temperature that the hot water poured on the hog froze before they could get him scraped. That is cold weather!

Once the hog was scalded, he was usually hung by his heels with a rope on a pulley attached to a big strong tree limb. At that point the butchering started. The belly was opened and the cleaning of the hog began. Hot water was again used to wash out the inside of the belly. The hog was placed on sawhorses with boards laid across them for the cutting-up stage. Portions of the backbones and ribs were carried to the house to be cooked for lunch and supper alongside a large pan of biscuits and some ribbon cane syrup to sop. The hams, shoulders, back strap, jowls, and middlings were carried to the smokehouse (behind locked doors) and laid on shelves to cool overnight.

Hog killings were usually a neighborhood event back in those days. Families came together to help one another with this big chore; sometimes neighbors assisted as well. Helpers were gifted with ribs, liver, and backbones for their families as payment for their help. Usually two large hogs were killed at the same time so there was plenty of meat to go around. Sometimes someone would want the hog's head and feet, and they were quite welcome to them as far as my mother was concerned. They would make what was called hogshead cheese that could be sliced and fried when it was seasoned up and got cold. Suppertime finally came and dark was well upon the little farmhouses where winter's meat was being prepared.

The next day, there was much more to be done. The meat that had gotten cold during the night was ready to be trimmed of fat and salted down. There was a "meat box" or barrel into which the cold meat was layered and packed with the salt preservative. The salt's job was to draw the water out of the meat and preserve it as the first part of the curing process began. After about a week, this meat would be removed and washed carefully in clear water to remove loose salt. Then it was ready for the smokehouse move.

The little smokehouse played a vital role in preserving and flavoring the meat for the family. The big hams, shoulders, bacon, and sausages would be hung from the rafters of the smokehouse, where a low fire was built with hickory wood and allowed to remain just a "smoke" while seasoning the beautiful meat to golden browns.

Meanwhile, the trimmings, along with maybe a shoulder or two, were cut into small pieces into big dishpans, where they would become sausages. The hand-powered meat grinder was attached to the end of the wooden dining table. One person fed the meat pieces into the grinder while turning the handle. Another person made sure there was a steady supply of meat on hand to grind. As the pile of ground-up meat grew, one pan would be removed and my mother or grandmother would dive in with their hands and mix up the sage, black and red pepper, salt, and other family favorite seasonings. When all was mixed to Mama and Granny's satisfaction, an iron skillet, hot on the wood stove, was filled with patties made from this fresh meat, tasted along the way to make sure the seasoning was just right. That was usually lunch, with a big pan of hot biscuits.

A special attachment was placed on the meat grinder and sausage casings were brought out to slip over the end of the attachment. Then the seasoned ground meat was fed through the grinder into the casings until a long string of stuffed sausages were obtained. The sausages were cut off and tied at the ends and ready to be hung in the smokehouse for curing. This was smoked sausage the homemade way. The smokehouse was filling up nicely.

I remember that when these jobs were completed, the kitchen was cleaned of scattered grease, the pans all washed and put away, the dining table cleaned from sausage-making, the sausage grinder washed and put away, and the wooden floors scrubbed. My tired granny and my mother would smile at each other. They were so tired they could hardly stand, but Granny would wipe her hands on her apron and say, "I'm so proud."

HOUSES OF THE PAST

Have you ever thought about the houses you've lived in in your lifetime? If you are young, probably you have not. If you are over fifty, you realize how much better off you are now as far as your place of abode than you were when you were a child.

The first memory I have of a house was a "shotgun mill house" in Pineland, Texas. In the late 1940s and early 1950s, Dad worked for Temple Lumber Company. We lived in a little two-bedroom sawmill house furnished by Temple for their workers for a small amount of rent. I do not know how much the rent was since I was just a little kid and was not worried about that sort of thing at that time.

The house was built with one room behind another straight back, thus the name "shotgun" house. The old saying was that you could shoot a gun from the front door to the back door without touching a thing! There were three rooms in that straight line: a living room, a middle bedroom, and a kitchen/dining in the back with small porches on each end of the house. A small side bedroom attached to the living room was the only other room. The outhouse was out back by the garden patch and the chicken yard. We did have running water, which was considered a great blessing by my mother. We had room at this place to have a small garden; a cow provided milk and butter and roamed the pasture belonging to somebody else behind us. We had a chicken yard and chicken house for Mama's chickens, who provided our eggs, and fried chicken on occasion.

According to tales I have heard, Mama and Daddy were very pleased to get this little house because up until then Daddy had to walk about four miles to work and back every day. That's right, I said FOUR MILES each way. We did not have a car then and not many other people did, either. When we were able to move to this house, we finally got a car of our own. We were moving up in the world.

We lived there until the summer of 1952, when we moved to Jasper. We found a rent house that was just a little better than the one we had in Pineland. It had indoor plumbing and a bathroom inside the house! It was a big deal. It had two bedrooms, a living room, and a kitchen, with porches on either end of the house as well. That house was sturdily built, and we had gas heaters to keep us warm in the wintertime and fans for the summer. We'd moved up again.

We rented another house for a few months when the owner of our first Jasper house needed to sell it. It was very similar, but we hadn't been there long before Daddy came home one day telling Mama he had found a place he wanted to buy. I think she was wondering where in the world he was going to find the funds to do that, but in those days, women didn't question. We drove out to Holly Springs to look at this place. Daddy said the house was little but had three acres of land and they only wanted a small amount for it. I don't remember the exact amount, but I was all excited over all this because Daddy was excited.

What I didn't realize was that he was trying to convince Mama that she would like it before we got there. When we drove up, I was not sure whether I liked it myself. It was an unpainted little house and my first ten-year-old impression was that it did not look as good as what we were living in. What was wrong with Daddy, anyway? I looked at Mama. Her brow had that familiar wrinkle in it that meant she was not real happy. She said nothing.

We got out and Daddy began showing her where the land lines were. It seemed very important to him that he owned some land of his own. We walked up the steps to the small front porch and into a tiny living room. There were five rooms total. Besides the living room, there was a dining room, a kitchen, two bedrooms, and no indoor bathroom. We were back to the rear of the house. Daddy was talking fast about painting the bare walls to make things look better until he could do some work on it. Mama looked with a nod. She opened the kitchen door to the small back porch and found the yard was a mess. It was filled with cans, bottles, and "stuff" that apparently had just been chucked out the back door. Now, you have to understand, my mama was a very clean, organized woman. She finally spoke.

"Well, this mess has got to be cleaned up." And her brown eyes snapped at Daddy. He nodded, seeming to know it was best not to talk now.

The more she looked, it seemed, the more she began to see it through different eyes. She said, "We could put some wallpaper up in the bedrooms, sheetrock the living room, get new linoleum for the floors first. Then there would have to be a sink in the kitchen and cabinets of some kind. Does it have water here?"

Daddy replied that it did have a shallow board well that had good water. She nodded. Then she said, "Well, it would be a start. Lots of work to do but we could do it."

That settled it. The house and three acres would be ours. Eventually, Daddy built a totally new house behind the little wooden shack he'd originally bought. It was a big house with three bedrooms, a living room, a dining room, a kitchen, a laundry room, and a bathroom, and it kept us warm until both my parents were gone to their heavenly home.

Even better than that, my husband and I built a house next door to them and raised our family in that same spot. Daddy had a vision of what it could be and made it happen. Sometimes things look bleak at the time, but if you have a vision of what it could be, with hard work and family love, it can be a wonderful thing.

LOVE MAKES IT REAL

Sometimes I can smell the wood in the fireplace as the pine kindling catches and blazes upward. The smoky, fresh odor of the fire, the sound of the crackling and sputtering of the red oak as it begins to blaze, still permeates my mind's senses. This time of year is when the first cool front comes blaring through East Texas, and as it changes our lives from heavy humid days to crisp, breezy autumn the smell gets stronger.

I can feel the warmth of the black iron stove in the corner of the kitchen and see the pipe routing the smoke out of the roof of the house on cold mornings. The iron skillet is sizzling on top of the black burner and is filled with large slices of ham cut from a sizable hunk of pork hanging from the rafters in the smokehouse. The pan of buttermilk biscuits is sending out an aroma that makes my saliva work overtime.

I hear sounds of stomping and scraping on the back porch as someone tries to clean mud off the soles of work boots. The screen door scrapes on the planks of the back porch and the wooden door creaks as it opens, bringing in the cold. He stands tall and lean, wearing blue overalls and a chambray shirt underneath a blue denim jacket. He carries a shiny aluminum bucket and all I can see is the white foam peeking over the top. The pail of warm milk is fresh from the Jersey cow now munching on feed in the cow lot by the barn. His graying hair is slipping out over his ears underneath the black felt hat that is as much a part of him as are the boots and overalls.

She quickly takes the pail and covers it with a clean dishtowel while she finishes breakfast. Her hair is bundled at the nape of her neck in a quickly assembled bun with wisps of long white hair flying about, softly framing her face, a face that is not wrinkled but simply shows signs of many years on life's journey. Over her cotton shirtwaist dress she wears a well-worn apron, covering the dress front with its bib and skirt and tied behind her small waist. She is not tall, but, watching her hands, I see strength in her arthritic fingers. When she looks up at me, her blue eyes smile and dance with love and good humor. She sets the hot pan of biscuits, along with the platter of ham, on a wooden board placed atop the oilcloth covering the table. The small dish filled with home-churned butter is already there, along with a glass filled with ribbon cane syrup made by one of the neighbors. It is a simple feast, one that is being served in many homes in East Texas this same morning.

I can hear the wind coming in strong, long gasps from the north as the cold envelops us. The large pecan trees that I so love to play under in the summertime are making loud creaking sounds as their bare limbs rub together, being pushed about by the wind. It could have sounded quite spooky, but to me it is not.

All this is more than sounds, smells, and feelings. What could it be? The house is not spacious, but quite small. The furniture is sparse and mostly homemade. Upon glancing about, one can conclude that only the bare necessities are there. That is all that is expected from life by them. So what is it that makes it all so special and makes me remember it so vividly all these years? What is it that makes me want to go back there and smell those smells, feel that warmth, and hear those sounds? Why is it that when I go back there and walk around, trying to bring it all back, I know it will never be the same and emptiness fills my heart? Why is it that I cannot hear the voices speak to me and feel the warmth, smell the breakfast, and hear the boots scrape on the back porch?

Then I realize that I can. I just did. It will never all be the same when I look at it today, but in my mind and in my heart it is still there. That's because love makes it real. It is just the way it was at Granny and Papaw's house on Manor Hill.

MY FIRST VACATION

The summer of 1949 was approaching and my little world was just fine. I was six years old that year and looking forward to a summer of playing and visiting Granny and Papaw and my cousins.

Daddy worked in the Dimension Plant at Temple Lumber Company in Pineland, Texas. We lived in a very small mill house in Pineland and had very little in the way of money. We had an old black Dodge coupe, and I have no idea what the year was but it was old in 1949! The idea of traveling very far in that automobile was unusual, but to a six-year-old, it did not matter much. Daddy could take care of anything, couldn't he? One day Mama told me that we were going on a little vacation with my aunt, uncle, and cousin.

In the first place, I had no idea what a "vacation" was, but if we were going with Aunt Mae, Uncle Odis, and Charles, I was all for it. They were a favorite aunt and uncle. Charles (my cousin in crime) and I had been known to stir things up when together ever since we were able to walk. He helped me get into some tight spots along life's way, or maybe it was the other way around!

June in Southeast Texas was hot, three-digits hot. Cars had no air-conditioning and neither did much else at that time. Plans were made and the two cars, ours and theirs, began our trek from their house in

Beaumont, Texas, to the ferry ride at Galveston. I was probably jumping up and down with excitement, talking as fast as I could and generally driving everyone crazy.

One has to remember that I was a little kid from Pineland, Texas, who was going the farthest away from home I had ever been. The biggest pool of water I had seen was McKim Creek in Sabine County, Texas. When we drove down to the beach of the Gulf of Mexico along Bolivar Peninsula, I was facing the biggest body of water I had ever seen. I stood there with my bare toes digging in the sand, the wind blowing my black hair in my face. There were fishermen with waders on out in the water a short distance, apparently watching the two cars of hillbillies from East Texas come crawling out and me silently watching the waves. One of the men came out of the water, probably to get more bait, and he spoke to my dad and me as we stood at the edge of the water.

"What do you think about that?" the man asked me.

I thought for a moment and answered with all the six-year-old wisdom I had. "It's a pretty big creek!"

When he finally stopped laughing, he turned to another fisherman nearby and said, "I wonder how big the rivers are where she comes from!"

I was worried when we got in sight of the ferry and realized we had to *drive* our car on that thing in the water. I began to whimper and worry. My mama wasn't very excited either, I noticed. Daddy said not to worry, it would be fine. He was grinning from ear to ear, as excited as a kid.

I lay down in the back seat and covered my head with my arms so I couldn't see what was happening when we crept onto the ferry. To my surprise, I did not even know when we were on the water instead of land, and when I lifted my head I could see we had made it on board. Daddy said when all the cars were loaded we could get out and look around while the ferry took us across to Galveston Island. It was June, remember. My parents were young, remember. They had never been on a "vacation" before either. So I scrambled out of the old Dodge, barefoot as a country girl could be, anxious to see what was happening. Daddy and Uncle Odis decided we should go up to the top level of the ferry so we could watch the seagulls swoop down on us. The steps leading up to the top were metal. It was June. Charles and I were barefoot. Off we went. Suddenly Charles and I started dancing around on the steps and crying and hollering. Our parents finally realized we were blistering our feet on those hot, hot steps. Daddy picked me up and Uncle Odis got Charles. They were embarrassed that they hadn't thought about our feet until we had already done damage. Actually, it did not blister our feet, but it did hurt and we played it to the hilt after we realized they felt bad about it.

We did not stay at the Galvez Hotel or any fine establishment. Our parents had rented a two-bedroom beach "house" perched on high piers near the beach. There was a small kitchen, a bathroom, and windows we could open and get the breeze from the Gulf of Mexico. We did not know we were uncomfortable because we were having too much fun. We went to the beach every day we were there and stayed until we were a crisp red. We ate hot dogs, Spam sandwiches, and whatever Mama and Aunt Mae could gather up for us. No restaurant eating, no fast-food places were in our vacation plan. There probably were not any and if there were, we would not have had the money to eat at them. We built sand castles, and played with the only beach ball we had. Our parents were young and played with us. It was fun and something I will always remember.

I wish parents today could realize that vacations do not have to cost a month's salary even today. The main thing is to spend time together, enjoying the earth we have been given to take care of and treasure, and playing together as a family. Time is the one gift you can give your family that is cheap, but more valuable than you will ever imagine. Go see all those big creeks in the world around you.

NEIGHBORS – AN OLD CONCEPT

In the twenty-first-century world, most people cannot tell you the names of the people who live across the street or in the house not ten feet away from their own. The world of mobility has caused us to pass one another with a wave as we back out of the driveway, at a school activity, or perhaps at the local grocery store. We do not know family backgrounds, work ethics, or how we believe on politics or religion. Not so back in the days of the 1940s and '50s.

The difference between then and now is largely that we lived in small communities back then and most of us were related in some way. When there was a new baby in the community, neighbors brought in food to help feed the family while Mama took care of the baby while enduring her "lying in." When the woman of the house became ill, a neighbor did her wash for her, and another came to wash dishes and sweep the house, make the beds and take care of the kids. Young girls who were big enough were taking care of younger children, cooking, and helping around the house. Boys were working alongside their fathers in the field, hoeing corn and cotton, feeding the animals, and milking cows. These are all things that will sound foreign to children of today.

I thought of some neighbors in my lifetime that I remember vividly for different reasons. You may have had some of these folks yourself.

The first was an elderly couple who lived beside us in a little mill-town house in Pineland, Texas, back in the 1940s. My mother visited often with the lady over the back fence while hanging clothes on the line to dry. They talked, knew a lot about one another, and became friends even though my mother was probably thirty years younger than this woman. What I remember about this lady was that she interfered in my life, much to my aggravation.

We had a porch swing on our front porch and this was where I played much of the time. The swing would become my car and I would line my dolls up in the swing and we'd travel all over the world in my imagination. I had my wagon on the porch and the dolls rode in the wagon as well. That was my playhouse and adults were really not needed as far as I was concerned.

One beautiful summer day, Mother hung her nylon hose on a little wire clothesline between the porch posts so they could dry. Women wore nylon hose that came up just to their knees and were held on by garters; no such thing as pantyhose back then. I was playing, Mama went back into the house, and I watched the nylons softly blowing in the breeze. They were so pretty, silky, thin so one could see through them, and I really needed to touch them. Since they hung down low enough for my short arms to reach them, I ventured over and ran my hands up into the hose. I was just feeling how soft and silky they were, not hurting one thing. That is when the neighbor lady got out of hand and came out on her front porch next door and hollered at me!

"Don't put your hands up in those hose, honey. You will ruin them." I took my hands down quickly, not because she told me to, but because she yelled so loudly that I knew Mama would be coming.

Sure enough, I heard the squeak of the screen door and Mama said, "What's going on out here?"

The lady next door quickly told Mama that she'd stopped me from ruining her nylons, like she had done something really big. I stood there very quietly with my hands behind my back, waiting.

Mama said, "Come on back in the house, Alene."

When we got inside, I had held back my frustration as long as possible.

"That ol' lady just sits over there watchin' me," I said. "She can't tell me what to do."

Mama sat down on the couch beside me and held the nylons in her hand. She gently put her hands up inside them like I'd done on the porch. Then she explained to me how easy it would be to pull a "runner" in them, ruining them so she could not wear them anymore. She said they cost money and we had to be careful with nice things that cost money. The neighbor was just thinking about me accidentally ruining the nylons, so she wanted me to stop, Mama said.

"Well I don't like her," I spouted. Mama smiled, patted me on the head, and told me she was a nice little lady and I did not need to say things like that. Then she made me sit on the couch, for a long time, it seemed to me. I never did like that lady after that, so when I played on the porch I would be exceptionally loud, thinking maybe I could annoy her!

Another neighbor lived on the other side of us in another mill-town house that looked just like ours. It was a man and his wife who were both hearing impaired. They could read lips or read signs, which people kind of made up to use to communicate with them. Eunice was the woman's name. She was young and pretty and could hear some but could not talk well. I have wondered since then if she had a cleft palate or something because it was difficult to understand her. But one thing I did understand was the love she had for children. She thought I was great. Now that was my kind of neighbor.

I loved music. Loved to sing and wanted to play a piano in the worst way. I was in the second grade at the time. The first time I visited Eunice's house with Mama, I discovered she had a piano – a really big, beautiful piano. My eyes lit up and I could hardly keep myself still because I wanted to touch it so badly. Finally, Eunice noticed and asked me if I wanted to play her piano. Did I? She sat on the piano stool with me and showed me Middle C. Then we played a little song using three notes. I was awestruck.

As time went on, Mama talked to Eunice about me taking piano lessons from a lady near us and asked if I could practice on Eunice's piano until they could get me one. Of course, I did not know any of this at the time. One day I came home and Mama said we were walking down the street to see someone. It was the music teacher lady. Mama told me I was going to start taking piano lessons and could use Eunice's piano to practice on until I had my own piano. I'm sure I levitated off the ground at least two feet!

Eunice loved having me come play her piano and allowed me all the time I wanted or needed to practice. Eunice could not read music; she'd just learned to play all by herself, so if I had questions about notes, she could not help me and I had to figure it out myself. I loved Eunice and her husband, who were super sweet to a little kid with big dreams.

The other neighbors I remember were actually neighbors of my grandparents in San Augustine County. They were elderly people and I called them Mr. Freeman and Miss Aggie. Back in those days, kids were not allowed to call adults by their first name unless you put "Mister" or "Miss" in the address. It was disrespectful and I would have had my backside tanned if I was disrespectful to an adult. What a difference from today.

My first cousin, Charles, and I stayed at Granny and Papaw's house together in the summer if our parents would let us. They were not so much worried about us as worried about whether my grandparents could stand us together for a week or two.

When we became bored in the afternoons and Granny was going to lie down and rest a little while, we would ask if we could go visit Mr. Freeman and Miss Aggie. They lived just out of sight of Granny's house but not far down the dirt country road. Granny usually let us because she needed the rest and quiet. Off we went to visit the neighbors. I don't know how old they were but they seemed really old to me and Charles. Mr. Freeman sat in his wooden rocking chair by the front window in the summertime. The front door would be open and there was no screen door so we could just walk on in. He would see us coming and start telling us to come right on in before we got the yard gate latched.

Mr. Freeman was not a tall man but he was sturdily built. We could tell that at one time in his youth, he was a force to be reckoned with. He'd worked hard in his day but now was crippled up in his legs and could not get around without his wooden cane. But he loved to talk and tell stories, and we were a captive audience.

Miss Aggie was not really too glad to see us I don't think. If she came out to visit at all, she was neatly groomed with her flower-print dress that came down to her ankles. Her hair must have been very long, but it was neatly arranged in a bun at the nape of her neck and was solid white. As a young woman, she must have been beautiful. Her house was spotless, except the spot on the floor next to Mr. Freeman's chair where he had a can into which he spit his snuff. Her beds were made with sparkling sheets and a pretty quilt folded at the foot.

I was never in any part of that house except the "fireplace room," or what we would call the living room. It had a bed, two or three wooden straight chairs, maybe a sewing machine, and a dresser of some sort. The floor was hardwood. It was untreated boards that were uneven and a faded gray color. There were no screens on the windows. The fireplace was the center focus of one wall. It was heat for the winter. In the summer, doors and windows were wide open and wasps and dirt daubers flew in at will.

We didn't care about any of the décor, but we were there to hear the stories that Mr. Freeman could tell about the days when San Augustine County was a bit wild – and apparently he was too! He was a great storyteller and we became spellbound as he talked and spit. The only instructions we ever got from Miss Aggie were to never touch the bed. She seemed to think we were a bit dirty with the smears of red dirt on our feet and legs. Of course, we were barefoot. Shoes were something only for Sundays and church during summer.

He told us stories about bringing goods from Nacogdoches to San Augustine along the El Camino Real with a wagon pulled by oxen. He brought axes, hoes, rakes, and yard and garden tools, as well as some clothing. He told of boxes of overalls and lots of hats. He especially remembered the many hatboxes he brought to San Augustine. He told about riding with the sheriff's posse to catch a cattle thief. He told about the Klu Klux Klan and how they ruled the countryside back in his youth. We were enthralled with his stories. The sad thing about all this is that I don't remember all the stories and I never wrote any of them down. Mr. Freeman has gone now and his stories are gone with him. That makes me very sad.

So what did I learn from these neighbors?

From the lady who kept me from ruining Mother's nylon hose, I learned that neighbors looked out for one another, even regarding nosy little kids.

From Eunice, the handicapped neighbor, who shared her love of music and piano with me, I learned that sharing brings joy to the giver and the receiver.

From Mr. Freeman, I learned the gift of storytelling, and that even dirty little kids always enjoy a good story. From Miss Aggie, I learned about being a graceful and clean lady who believed in keeping a clean house even in hard times.

Neighbors taught me a lot and I hope I am always a good neighbor. When some dirty little kids come visit me, I hope I have time to share, teach, and tell a good story.

POLITICS AND ELECTION NIGHT

CAN YOU REMEMBER THE WAY it was on election night in the 1940s and '50s? Television did not play a very big part in elections and politics back then because very few people in East Texas had a television. We were still in the world of radio and newspapers. Word of mouth flew about with the power of dynamite; however, much of it was not true. Sometimes news was old by the time we got it back here in the deep green forests of Southeast Texas.

Local politics was big stuff back then, as it is today. There were some viciously fought battles over sheriff races in Sabine, San Augustine, Jasper, and Newton Counties. Feelings ran strong along the banks of the Sabine, Neches, and Angelina rivers, and feuds were rampant in some areas at this time.

People sat out on their galleries (front porches) late in the evening after a hard day's work watching evening fade into night, talking about the upcoming election. Neighbors walking home after their day of labor at a neighboring farm stopped, sat down on the edge of the porch to rest a bit, and the talk of a hot local sheriff's race began. That neighbor was offered a cool drink of water from the water bucket on the water shelf. He commented on the good taste of their well water as he drank from the gourd or tin dipper that everyone in the family used. It was a good time and lots of problem-solving took place on galleries around the countryside.

Politicians traveled about the county in an old jalopy, in a pickup, or, in earlier years, on horseback, paying a visit to little farms along the way. If they saw the farmer out plowing in his field, they stopped to solicit his vote and tell him all their plans to improve the county roads, bring peace to the countryside, and make life safer for all. Most of it was done with grace and Southern hospitality. Some of it was not.

Tempers could flare at the drop of a hat, and sometimes fistfights were used to settle these disagreements. There were a few times when guns were drawn and perhaps used to make a point. It was an unsettled part of Texas, for a large part, until the late 1950s and early 1960s. We were settled in the strip of Texas between the Sabine River dividing us and Louisiana and the Calcasieu River in Louisiana. For many years in early Texas history, there was no law. It was called the "neutral ground"; however, there was nothing neutral about it. The law was everybody's wishes and nobody was in charge. The people who were running from the law in Louisiana drifted across the Sabine River into the neutral ground to escape whatever sheriff was chasing them. Every man for himself, and those who were good, law-abiding citizens had to protect themselves the best way they could. Most fireplace mantles were graced with a double-barrel shotgun mounted above for handy use, along with a box of shells.

This was all taking place less than one hundred years after the Civil War. Feuding was prevalent and unforgotten battles had not been finished. So election night could be a good night to even the odds in some cases.

I was a child under ten years old during the early 1950s. When election night came around, my dad wanted to go to Hemphill (the county seat for Sabine County) to watch the results come in on the courthouse square as the election boxes came in. When I was small, Mother and I sat in the car and Daddy went up on the square to watch the numbers being put up on the big chalkboard by the courthouse door. The voting boxes from every little rural box in the county were being brought into the courthouse to be counted. It took a while to get them all in, verified, and approved and for the counting to begin. Chairs and benches were brought outside from the courthouse so ladies and the elderly folks could sit comfortably and visit while waiting. The gathering on the square was well attended and as they discussed their opinions, sometimes these erupted into severe disagreements.

Daddy wanted to know about the presidential vote and the sheriff's vote. Also he was interested in the Texas governor's race. I wanted to get out and run and play but my parents said I had to stay in the car. I could not understand their reasoning then but I know now there were fights breaking out on the square, people were drinking and boozing it up, and bad language was spoken and my daddy was not about to let me out in that atmosphere.

Later in the early 1950s, things calmed down a bit and I could run and play on the square with the passel of kids running wild in that area, but when Daddy thought things might be heating up, he rounded me up pretty quick and said it was time for us to go home.

Politics has always been a touchy subject and every person has an opinion, as they should. But in those early days when everybody had a shotgun in his truck, a knife in his pocket, and a pistol on his belt or inside his blue-jean jacket, it could turn bad in a hurry.

Has anything changed much since then until the present day, 2016? Due to television and news traveling much faster than it did then, elections are predicted and winners declared within hours of the close of the polls. National television reporters declare winners almost by the time the polls have closed in some parts of the country. Back in the 1940s and 1950s, voters must wait until late in the night to get a trending of how the vote was going. Sometimes it was days before a president could be declared winner and the news got back to our part of the Texas countryside. But the flared tempers, opinionated folks, and harsh words are still the same. Not all the changes are good, but all of it is part of the growth of our country. I miss the camaraderie of the small communities that used to be. I still love those memories of the way it was.

SINGING BIRDS

By Alene Dunn
September 2012

Author's Note: One morning I was sitting on my patio drinking coffee, doing my morning prayers, and listening to the noises of my country home. The rain began to slowly fall and the birds were nestling up in the pear tree by my house. I wrote this for my granddaughters (Allie and Olivia Dunn) so they would never forget the beauty of God's sounds.

I hear the birds singing, as the rain comes falling down.
Wonder what they're saying, if their happiness abounds?
Are they saying, "Thank you, Father, for the rain this day"?
Or complaining of wet feathers and why it happened this way.

No, I think they're singing praises, to the Father up on high.
They'll find more bugs and insects 'cause the rain is coming by.
We must always thank the Father for all blessings we receive,
Then, like the singing birds, thanks for the blessings our Heavenly Father leaves.

SLEEPING PORCHES AND DOG TROTS

IF YOU'VE NEVER SLEPT ON a sleeping porch, a dog-trot, or a front porch, you have missed a treat. A sleeping porch was a screened-in porch furnished with a bed or two in the summertime to make a cool place to sleep. In the Southern states, the three-digit temperatures, along with the terrible humidity, made sleep a difficult thing in the days before fans or air-conditioning. Most houses had wide porches across the front and back of their houses. Their ingenuity kicked in and they screened in the porch and moved beds out there when the summer nights became unbearable in the house. At bedtime, the whole family could bed down out on the porch and the screen prevented bugs and mosquitoes from taking bites. It also gave some protection from wild animals who roamed about at night. The farmer and his family could rest their tired bodies after a hard day in the fields. Children were not allowed to play on the sleeping porches during daytime unless it was raining and they were unable to go outside. If they were caught with their dirty bodies or feet on those pearly white sheets, they were in big trouble.

Some people lived in dog-trot houses. Those were homes built with a large, wide hall in the middle of the structure with rooms opening up onto the hall from either side. Usually the fireplace room, as it was called, and the kitchen/dining area was on one side and a bedroom or two on the other side.

At the very back was what was generally called a "shed room," where more expensive tools and equipment might be kept.

In summer, beds were moved into the dog-trot breezeway and people slept there. There was no screen to protect you so mosquitoes had a field day, but at least it was cooler. Sometime, a fire was built in the yard so the smoke would cause the mosquitoes to go away for a while. Meanwhile, there seemed to always be a breeze in the middle of a dog-trot house.

My great-uncle had such a house. I spent at least a week there every summer up in San Augustine County visiting with cousins. We played in the dog-trot all the time until Aunt Artie ran us outside. We would play hide-and-seek and go tromping through that hallway full speed ahead, making way too much noise to be hiding. When she got tired of it, she put us out. When it was hot after lunchtime, we sat around on the porch telling yarns, playing jacks, giggling, laughing, and being generally obnoxious. Sometimes, Uncle Lonnie would go to the store by catching a ride with someone (he did not have a car), and if he could not catch a ride back he had to walk probably five miles to get home. He would bring us ice cream if he caught a ride back so it would not melt before he got there. We would be giddy with excitement because that was a supreme treat. The thing was, Uncle Lonnie liked ice cream as much as we did, so he filled his need for cold sweetness as well as ours. We settled down on the edge of the porch, swinging our dirty bare feet and savoring every precious mouthful of the ice cream.

My grandparents did not have a sleeping porch, but they had a wide front porch across the entire front of their house. Once when I was there in the summer along with a first cousin two years younger, we made great plans. We planned all day long to sleep on the front porch that night. We planned to put quilts down for pallets and bring our pillows and a sheet for cover from the mosquitoes and watch the fireflies until we went to sleep. We asked Granny if we could do that and she said she guessed it would be all right. When we sat down to the lunch table, my papaw came in from the field for his lunch break and we happily told him our plans. He kept on eating silently, not saying a word for a long time. When he finished eating, he looked up at us and said, "I guess it will be okay, unless a possum or coon decides to walk up on the porch to see who you are out there."

Our eyes got big as saucers and we lost our appetite immediately. I asked, "They wouldn't come up on the porch," giggling like it was some kind of joke. Papaw was always pulling things on us anyway.

"Well, they get in the chicken house pretty regular, along with that old fox that likes those little chickens out there. Why, I killed a possum out there just last week. They might come check you out. They probably wouldn't hurt you, but I just thought it might scare you two city slickers," he said without a smile.

My cousin Charles had not said a word, but now he rose to the occasion. "Well, I'll have my slingshot and pistol out there right by my pallet. I'll give 'em something that'll run 'em off." He thought he was Roy Rogers at the time. He was indeed the confident eight-year-old male.

Papaw got up and went out on the porch, where he turned down a straight-back chair to rest the back of the chair on the floor. That was where he took a short nap every day before returning to the field. We got through eating and went outside on the other side of the house so as not to bother him. I felt we needed to talk.

"I'm not sleeping out there with wild animals messing around," I said.

"Aw, that won't happen. He's just pullin' our legs," my brave cousin said.

The cautious female said, "Well, I'm not sleeping out there. You can if you want to but you'll do it by yourself. I'm not doing it!"

By the time bedtime came around, I had decided I would make me down a pallet right in front of the screen door that led out to the porch and sleep right there. I would get some breeze but there was a screen between me and the wild animals. Charles was determined to sleep on the porch, or so he said. We all made preparations for bed. I put down my pallet, I got my pillow, and I was ready to sleep. Charles kept fooling, around finding excuses to not go make his bed down on the porch. Finally, Papaw said he'd go help Charles fix his bed because it was time we all went to bed. They went out on the porch and I lay down on my pallet. I could hear them talking but not what they said.

In a few minutes, they came in and Papaw went on to his bed while Charles and his quilt came into the room where I was lying on my pallet. He began spreading his quilt beside mine.

"What are you doing? Why are you sleeping in here?" I asked.

"Well, I thought since you was scared, I'd just sleep in here with you." He sheepishly looked at me.

I let it go. I was sleepy, but I secretly snickered to myself because I knew he was not as brave as he thought he was.

SCHOOL DAYS

By Richmond Pierce Veatch

Author's Note: Richmond Pierce Veatch was my uncle I never met. He died at a young age, but he left for us the poetry near and dear to his heart. He was, from the accounts of his siblings, a creative, musical fellow who would have accomplished much had his health been good. I wanted to share his work here for all to enjoy. I wish I had known him.

The sun again rising
O'er the majestic hills and dells
And I hear again the ringing
Of the distant faithful bells.

'Tis time to start to school again
The place I love so dear.
And tread the meadow pathway
Through the morning atmosphere.

The time I spend in going to school
Will be just like a dream
When I look back o'er the fleeting years
That in my memory gleam.

I have learned quite many things
Which to me is very great.
How the greatest of our heroes
Met with their awfull fate.

I have learned about how Washington
Crossed the Delaware.
O'er the crest of the frozen water
With iceburghs floating there.

I have learned about Lee and Jackson
How they won the battles of fame
And upon the pages of history
Will ever be written their name.

In the valley of Shenandoah
The tide of battle soared.
And for the cause of truth and right
The faithful cannons roared.

In the silent and lonely valley
Where the brave heroes lay
Has fluttered the starry emblem
And zephyrs of paradise played.

I've heard the song and story
And it still appeals to me.
Of the March of General Sherman
From Atlanta to the sea.

And in my mind still lingers
The flash of the soldiers' eye
As they rallied 'round the ensign
That towered in the sky.

SEVEN LITTLE FACES

By Alene Dunn (September 21, 2014)

Author's Note: This poem was written after a family gathering when my granddaughters and adopted grandchildren (from my daughter-in-law's family) were all together. We blended well, with many colors of skin combined with wonderful personalities. Precious little souls that mean the world to me.

I stare out my window and look to the sky
Seven little faces shine in my mind's eye.
Each one is different and so full of life
I pray that this world won't fill them with strife.

The two little dark skins pass ever so fast
Their black hair and eyes shimmer in light gently cast.
They laugh and play as they glance at me
My love for them I happily see.

The two little boys with a light tan skin
Both are so different, but precious within.
They call me Grammy and make my heart swell
I pray my influence in their lives will dwell.

Then there's little sister all smiles and beauty
Who captured my heart and is such a cutie.
She's just turned two but what will her future bring?
I know she will do much and make my heart sing.

The last two are those who share my last name.
The two who give life meaning, make lonely days wane.
The blond with blue eyes that look like Big Pop's
So smart and sweet and climbs to the top.

The dark-haired beauty with personality galore
Reminds me of her dad, we wonder what's in store.
Her grin and her beauty will carry her far
But her sweet loving heart I pray can't be marred.

Thank you, God, you've blessed me so much
With seven little faces that I can touch
What would life be without these beautiful faces
That fly in my sky and share different places.

SPRING TIME

Written March 10, 1924
By Richmond Pierce Veatch

The birds are singing sweetly
To welcome the beautiful spring.
And the wind blows low and silent
O'er the fields of waxing grain.

The tall green grass is waving
Beneath the warm blue sky.
And the leaves on the trees hang trembling
As the wind goes passing by.

How sweet is the hour that brings release
From the cold mid-winter days
And gives to us the blossoming flowers
And the warm sunshine of May.

The beautiful song of springtime
Is the sweetest song of all
When we hear the distant echo
Of the glistening waterfall.

The odor of flowers is everywhere
And insects sporting and birds awing.
The thrush has come with a song and a cheer
And all seems to hail the coming of spring.

O! 'Tis beyond my power to paint
The minstrel of nature in harmony bland.
Ye are dearer by far to the poet than all
The beautiful landscapes imposing and grand.

The halo of nature is in the air
With the pathos of love and the birds that sing.
So let us all join in the chorus so grand
And help sing the beautiful song of Spring.

SUMMER PLACE

I remember my summer place
Soft breezes gently touching my face.
I remember feeling the soft red sand
So cool and silky in my hand.
The days were bright with joy and fun
I never once noticed the sun.
Corn stalks rustled as the breeze went by
Birds chirped happily in the sky.
My own little world lived there in my mind
In my place of peace and nothing unkind.
My knees were dirty through and through
My heart was clean like the morning dew.
There in my soul where I grew up from a child
Learned about nature and things worthwhile.
Those times are gone and can ne'er be replaced,
Because they are still there in my summer place.

UNCLE CHESTER AND AUNT VIE

Perhaps the most colorful aunt and uncle in my family were Aunt Vie and Uncle Chester. She was raised in Blackjack with the rest of the Sam and Nan Veatch bunch, but somehow she turned out a little different. She maintained a sense of "entitlement" which she expected from all the other siblings. The story from her brothers and sisters was that Papa (Sam Whitson Veatch) caused the whole thing because she was his favorite child. Now, I don't know anything about it for sure because it happened long before I got here, but I do know Aunt Vie was a little demanding.

She was married in her twenties to Chester, who was a full-fledged Cajun from West Lake, Louisiana. They lived in Orange, Texas, for a while. Uncle Chester worked at the shipyard during World War II and Aunt Vie stayed home reading her romance books. She loved those romance books and it was reported that her reading caused lots of trouble as a young girl at home when chores were not done.

Like most of the Veatch kids, she had coal-black hair and a ready grin, loved to garden, loved her flowers, and tended to be a bit on the lazy side. According to the women of the family, Viola got by with much when she was a child and thus it caused a fracas when she was an adult.

Aunt Vie and Uncle Chester never had children. But she liked children and was fun to play with when I was little. She always brought me some little gift when they came to visit and I thought she was a pretty neat lady. We got along just fine as I grew up, but things began to change as I got older. I think she changed with age and I grew to realize that she'd changed.

She never could get along with her brothers and sisters. At Christmas dinners when the family was all together and presents were exchanged, everybody was proud and grateful for their presents…except Aunt Vie. She never liked what she got and usually let everyone know it. She was not very good at hiding her thoughts and opinions, so somebody's feelings were hurt. She and my daddy tied up on a regular basis. He challenged her straightforward opinions and attempted to teach her some graceful actions. It didn't work.

But then, you have to remember, this woman had six brothers who tormented her royally. You see, they resented Papa's allowing Vie to get away with things for which they got spanked. She probably held it over their heads that Papa wouldn't let anybody touch her because she was special.

At Christmas they would lure her outside, where they had a big fire built and all the guys were crowded around popping firecrackers. As soon as she got outside, they would set off a fire chaser under her feet, making her dance, scream, run, and jump. One time, they pulled such a stunt and she jumped the fire to get away from the chaser with her coattail flapping in the wind and the boys all bending double with laughter. So you can see that part of her problem was her brothers.

But Aunt Vie didn't like her sisters either. She accused them of thinking they were better than her. When she sewed herself a new dress and one of the sisters would compliment her on it, she later would say they were making fun of her. She knew they must be talking behind her back because they thought they could sew better than she. Of course, it was all in her head, but very real to her.

One time she went fishing with her brother, Virgil, who came over every summer with his family from New Orleans to East Texas. He loved coming back home to his roots and he dearly loved to fish. He asked Aunt Vie if she knew how to get back to Devil's Ford, a little creek he had fished many times as a young man. She said she did, not realizing that due to the building of Sam Rayburn Dam, many roads had been changed or closed off. They started out on their fishing adventure, both happy to relive some old memories. Aunt Vie was giving directions but when they came up to where she thought the creek should be it was not there. Uncle Virgil said, "Well, Vie, we must be at the wrong place. Where do I go now?"

To which she replied with great indignity, "Well, it is supposed to be here. They must have moved it!"

Uncle Chester worked all his life at sawmills around the Jasper, Texas, area. He could spit out words in his regular conversation that I had never heard much before. He cursed as a matter of speaking. I remember asking Daddy one time why he talked like that and he told me that Uncle Chester was not being ugly, it was just the way he grew up talking. Using bad language and curse words was normal to him. He did not realize most of the time he was doing it. He drank lots of strong Seaport coffee, black. His coffee and self-rolled cigarettes were a part of his life every time you saw him. He loved Western-type movies. Every time the Texas Theater in downtown Jasper got a new Western, he and Aunt Vie were right there to see it. He called them "shoot 'em ups" and loved them every one. He suffered a major heart attack one day while working at a Jasper-area sawmill, and it took his life.

I loved Aunt Vie and Uncle Chester. In her later years, Aunt Vie fell to the dementia that plagued many of the siblings. She became blind from glaucoma, finishing her life in a nursing home, where she began to mellow a little. I will always remember her as someone who was a lot of fun, someone who obviously had some problems primarily because her father treated her differently, plus the resentment of her brothers and sisters.

She's long since gone to her reward and there she will find peace and rest. I'm not sure she'll find any romance novels there, though. But that's just the way she was.

UNCLE LONNIE AND AUNT ARTIE

Uncle Lonnie was my papaw Worry's brother. He and Aunt Artie lived in the little community of New Hope between San Augustine and Nacogdoches, Texas. During the summer, that was one of my favorite places to be. They had three adult children and two that were close to my age. My first cousin, Charles, and I, along with Uncle Lonnie's youngest two children, Lonnie Ray and Lela Mae, were like stair-steps in age. I was the oldest, Lonnie Ray was the youngest, Lela Mae and Charles were in the middle. We all wound up at New Hope together during the summer for a week. I cannot imagine how much havoc we could initiate in that week!

Their house was an old-fashioned dog-trot-style house with a wide hall down the middle open to a porch that ran all across the front of the house with steps going into the back yard on the back. There were two rooms on either side of the dog-trot. One side had a "fireplace room," where Uncle Lonnie and Aunt Artie slept and wooden chairs were placed in front of the fireplace for visiting. There were two beds in that room and if it was too cold, the children could sleep in there near the heat as well. The other room on that side was the kitchen and dining area combined.

Aunt Artie's kitchen had a black wood stove taking up one corner. In the summer, the stove made the little room unbearably hot. There was no electricity there in those days, only kerosene lamps. In winter, the stove heated up that side of the house with its warmth. There was no running water, no sink. But a washpan and a water bucket filled with water drawn from their well outside with a tin dipper sat on a homemade wooden shelf. She got her cooking water from that bucket and we were supposed to use the pan to put water in and wash our hands. Sometimes that had to be forced upon us.

A wooden dining table stood along the opposite wall, surrounded by a wooden bench on the back side and home-made wooden ladder-back chairs on the other sides. The old food safe was there too, holding her "good" dishes, bowls, and food that had been previously prepared to keep it away from flies and bugs flying around. The table was covered with an oilcloth, with some kind of design on it, that could be wiped off after each meal.

The kitchen leaned downhill at a considerable angle from the fireplace room. Apparently the sills may have been failing underneath it, or it was just sinking on the back side of the house. I do not know why it did that but it was always that way in my memory. So if you sat on the bench behind the table, you were kind of pitched forward toward the downhill side. If you were seated in a chair on the opposite side of the table, you were leaning backward away from the table and had to reach uphill to eat. Seems funny to think of it now but that is the way it was.

At mealtime, one could expect a large pitcher of sweet iced tea, plenty of milk, and cornbread hot from the stove with lots of cow butter ready to adorn it. Fresh peas or beans from the field, corn on the cob, perhaps fried okra or stewed potatoes, red juicy sliced tomatoes, and fresh green onions from the garden. Always there was something sweet for desert. You see, Uncle Lonnie had a sweet tooth and Aunt Artie managed to keep something on hand for her man. Sometimes she had sugar cookies (or teacakes), chocolate pie, caramel pie made from caramelized brown sugar, egg custard pie, or maybe coconut cake. Aunt Artie was one of the best cooks to be found in New Hope and probably most of the area around the Attoyac River.

She was a short little woman who wore her graying hair in a bun at the nape of her neck. She worked hard in the field and hard in the house and talked most of the time she did it. She was a strong woman in character and I can best describe her as being a genuinely good person to the core.

I'm sure Aunt Artie was a good woman, or she would have killed us kids before we ever got grown. Some of the things we did were awful for those days. Things like staying up giggling until all hours of the night or until Uncle Lonnie yelled, "Do you want me to come over there? Go to sleep."

Now if you have never been in a dog-trot house, let me tell you that on the hottest of days, if there was a breeze anywhere it would find its way down the dog-trot. Theirs had a narrow cot on the porch with a quilt on it and usually a pillow. Sometimes after lunch, Uncle Lonnie lay on the cot for a rest before going back to work. He did carpentry work and all kinds of light jobs for people around the area.

Of course, while he was trying to rest a bit, we were running like wild cowboys through the dogtrot, playing chase, hide-and-seek, or cops and robbers. I guess he tuned us out, because he never threatened us that I remember. He always had a good sense of humor and loved to joke around with us. He also enjoyed having good things to eat and many times in summer evenings, he came home with the ingredients needed to make ice cream and maybe a borrowed ice cream maker. The kind you turn with a handle. That was when he was our very best friend.

Another one of our incidents was when we played a trick on the boys. They dealt us lots of misery so it was our turn to get them. We put two straight-backed chairs lined up, leaving a space in the middle so it looked like there were three chairs there when there was really only two.

Lela and I carefully draped a quilt over the whole thing and pretended it was a couch. We told them we were going to have a play and they were our audience, inviting them into the bedroom where we girls slept to sit down and get ready for our play – on our "couch." Charles came in first and, being as lucky as could be, he sat down in the middle where there was no chair. He knocked over both chairs and hit the floor himself with a bang. Aunt Artie came rushing in to see if anyone was hurt while Lela and I were bent over laughing. Needless to say, Charles was not happy with us, and threatened to beat us up and all that stuff.

The boys' favorite thing to do was pester us when we went to the outhouse. There was no bathroom or toilet in the house, so one had to go to the two-hole outhouse. We went out there just to get away from them! One day we snuck out there so we could talk about them and they figured out where we went. So they started throwing dirt clods at the outhouse. So we yelled at them to stop, to which they dared us to come get them. We let them wear themselves out throwing dirt clods and then begged them to let us out. We opened the door and they were standing close by, so then the chase began!

This foursome played hopscotch, jump rope, jacks, chase, and hide-and-seek, shelled peas and made messes. But my, what memories we made on these summer days at Uncle Lonnie and Aunt Artie's. We entertained ourselves without electricity, no video games, no television, no radio, and no electronic games. Just us and the world around us is how we played. We still love to remember those times and how much we miss Uncle Lonnie and Aunt Artie from New Hope, Texas.

UNCLE MATT AND AUNT HATTIE

ONE OF THE NEAT THINGS about going to Granny and Papaw's was the other relatives living nearby to visit as well. Just about my favorite other place to go was to Aunt Hattie and Uncle Matt's house. Aunt Hattie was my dad's oldest sibling and one of his favorites.

Just about my most un-favorite thing about getting to their house was that muddy dirt road. It was even worse than Manor Hill! When it rained, that road was practically impossible to travel in a car. A tractor could manage it pretty well and was used quite often to pull people out of the ditches or just out of that sticky, deep mud. The ruts became so deep in the red mud that the bottom of the car dragged on the center in between the tire tracks. And you were really in a pickle if you met someone else. There was only one set of ruts and you had better try to stay in them. Either you or the other fellow you met had to back up, or the only other option was to get out of the ruts. That's when you sank. I always hated muddy roads.

Another real fun part of going down that road was the bridge with no banisters. It was, of course, a wooden bridge, amounting to boards nailed across some rails over a pretty deep ravine with a tiny stream of water running through it most of the time. When it rained, that tiny stream could burst out of its banks and flood the cotton fields surrounding it on either side. Whether it was flooded or dry as a bone, I just knew we would fall off that bridge into the little creek.

Because my dad was always part kid, the muddy road was a challenge to him. The old Dodge coupe he drove was tough and he pushed it through that mud without too many problems most of the time. When we got stuck, we walked to Aunt Hattie's house and Dad and Uncle Matt came back with the tractor and pulled the car out of the mud and to the house. Dad thought it was great fun. I did not.

At this time, Uncle Matt was a cotton farmer. As times changed and he got older, he changed his livelihood to raising chickens for poultry houses. It was a profitable and prevalent way to make a living in the early 1950s in San Augustine and Shelby Counties. Everyone wanted to get in on the action, and long tin chicken houses sprang up everywhere. Uncle Matt had such chicken houses. The most memorable thing to me about the chicken houses was that they stank! I always felt sorry for the little chickens all cooped up in that hot chicken house and squawking for dear life. Uncle Matt raised and sold many hundreds of chickens during this time.

Prior to the chicken-house venture, in addition to raising cotton, he raised corn (for feed for the animals) and had a large garden to supply their own food. There were a few small houses down on the little branch behind his house where some of his workers lived and worked for him, picking, planting, and taking care of the crops.

Uncle Matt was a short, thin man, probably not over five and a half feet tall. He moved with rapid short steps as though to get the work done quickly. He always wore a hat and khaki shirt and pants, dipped his snuff, and stuttered. It took him three minutes to get out words like "town," "Murry," "money," etc. He gestured with his hands as though to bring the words out of his mouth but it did not seem to help much. My dad always said that when Uncle Matt got angry he did not have any trouble with stuttering. I never saw him mad so I just have to take Dad's word for that part.

Uncle Matt was a mischievous, funny little man who enjoyed joking and picking on folks he really liked. He enjoyed aggravating me when we came because I usually obliged him by giving him the result he was looking for. I bit at everything he threw my way. This tickled him good because I'd try my best to think of something smart to say and he always out-did me. I was about ten to twelve years old during this time so I was geared up for a fight and he loved to give it to me. An example of his baiting me went something like this.

We always had an old car that would just barely run. It seemed every time we went to San Augustine and Denning, we had a flat or it broke down or wouldn't crank after we arrived or something happened. Uncle Matt used to tell Daddy when we were getting ready to leave his house, "Well, Murry, y-y-you'd b-b-better get s-s-started. That ol' c-car m-m-may need s-s-some of my h-h-haywire to hold it t-t-together!"

Then I'd chime in with true assurance that our car was not going to need any of his old haywire and that we could manage just fine without it.

He also enjoyed accusing me of having all my dresses made from feed sacks. Back then, feed for the animals came in big bags made of cotton material with flowered designs printed on it. Mother and Granny would save up enough of the same prints to make dresses from them. It was good material and times were hard. Nothing was wasted, thus some of my dresses did come from feed sacks, but for some reason my pride got in the way and I did not like to admit it. Uncle Matt delighted in asking me whenever we arrived if that dress I had on was made out of feed sacks. I would immediately rise to the occasion and inform him plainly that my dress was *not* made from any old cow or horse feed sack and that it was "store bought" material. He thoroughly enjoyed these little episodes, and little did I realize then that I enjoyed them too.

Then there was Aunt Hattie. Where Uncle Matt was short, Aunt Hattie was tall, regal, and beautiful. As a young woman she had black hair, thick and beautiful. As I remember her, it had begun to show a smattering of gray. She kept her house neat and clean – at least as neat as she could with Uncle Matt tromping in and out wearing muddy boots. She liked nice, pretty things in her house and took good care of them. She had a great sense of humor as well and loved joking around. But to me, she was always kind, soft, smiling, and full of love.

The Veatch clan generally met for Christmas at Aunt Hattie and Uncle Matt's house. Grandma Veatch lived with her children in her last years, moving from place to place. She somehow always managed to be at Aunt Hattie's for Christmas, thus all the family came to wherever she was. The atmosphere at Christmastime there at Aunt Hattie's house was something I will never forget.

The big Christmas tree was the focal point of the living room, taking up a large corner area. It was a cedar cut down from the woods around the property. Uncle Matt could always find a tree that was bigger than the space in the living room, but he brought it in anyway. Decorations were slim during those days; silver garland or perhaps a red garland was all that adorned the tree. No fancy glass balls, no expensive hangings were to be found on this tree, but when I walked into that living room with big eyes and great excitement, it looked wonderful to me. Uncle Matt was the great decorator at Christmas. He loved to have all the family there and he loved Christmas. Besides the tree, he went out in the woods and found some pretty green vines of some sort. He brought them in, mounting them all around the tops of the walls of the room. Sometimes there were pine boughs over the fireplace and doorways of the room as well. It really smelled like Christmas!

While he worked on the decorations in the living room, the kitchen was Aunt Hattie's domain. The aroma of delicious things being prepared hit one's nose immediately upon stepping into the house. That was my favorite place to be before lunch was served, but I tended to get in the way. Mother sat me at the big dining table to watch Aunt Hattie put the white fluffy icing on her four-layer coconut cake. My dad always called that icing "calf slobber icing" and did not like it much. It was really called seven-minute icing, made primarily from beaten egg whites and sugar.

One of my other aunts would be peeling and cutting up fruit for fruit salad in a gigantic bowl. I watched that procedure and was given a bite of apple or orange as it progressed toward completion. Every family member who came in had a box of food in their arms. Those boxes were filled with ham, deviled eggs, pies, sweet potatoes with marshmallows melted on top, and on and on. Mama was in the kitchen making dressing. Aunt Hattie had the old hen already cooked and cornbread made and she and Mama mixed up this big roasting pan of chicken dressing. There was a lot of discussion on the seasoning of the dressing. It had to be just right and they always nailed it! Aunt Hattie's butane stove oven was hot and ready to let the dressing come together for our feast.

I always thought when I saw the dressing pan come out of the oven that we were ready to eat – but not so. The homemade yeast rolls or biscuits, whichever we had, went into the oven to bake first. I thought I would die from suspense waiting for all these goodies to get ready. I knew we couldn't open all those presents piled up under the tree until after dinner. It was torture!

The men were outside, usually standing around a little fire they had built out there. They were talking, telling yarns, and someone would reach into their pocket and bring out the firecrackers. Then the noise started. They would laugh and pop firecrackers until dinner was ready.

After lots of eating, laughing, joking, and catching up on family news, it was time to gather in the living room around the Christmas tree. This was what I had been waiting for all day long! There were a few times, when money was scarce, that we drew names for the following year's gifts. Everybody got Grandma something so she had a big, big stack to open.

Mama and Daddy usually put a gift under that tree for me as well as whoever got my name. Sometimes Uncle John and Aunt Leona got me something too. Of course, Aunt Vie never liked what she got and everyone got something better than she did (according to her), but all just went on their merry way and let her mutter to herself. Afterward, her brothers had been known to take her outside after the presents were opened and put a firework or two chasing after her. She didn't like that either.

The gifts were all things we needed. Not many frivolous things were given. Money was scarce and could not be frittered away on things we did not need. Usually every person got some kind of clothing because that was always needed. Socks, handkerchiefs, and possibly a work shirt for the men; nylon hose, homemade aprons, embroidered dishtowels, or kitchen tools were what the women received. I usually got material to make me dresses. Mother was always happy but I always kept looking for just a toy. Aunt Leona and Uncle John sometimes gave me a coloring book or a book to read and that was my most favorite gift.

After the mess was cleaned up, the wrapping paper was carefully folded and put away to be used next year; bows were saved as well to be reused. Then it was time for music. Aunt Hattie had an old pump organ in her living room and I would get over there to it. Uncle Cecil got his guitar and Uncle Matt pulled out his old fiddle. It was time for playing, singing, and wonderful times.

We were big on family gatherings at Christmas, and the ones I remember most from my dad's family were those at Aunt Hattie and Uncle Matt's. It was a tradition as long as Grandma was alive, and afterward I kept that tradition up at my house until most all my aunts and uncles were gone. Make some traditions today in your family that your children will hold on to all their lives. These traditions will give them a smile as life goes by.

TALES OF THE CHICKEN YARD

When I was a little girl, about three or four years old, Mother took me out to the chicken yard to feed the chickens every evening. She scattered corn about in the yard while the hens and their children scuffled about, trying to get more than the next one.

One day while we were feeding, one of the old hens spotted the tiny little buttons on the front of my dress. She apparently thought it was a new kind of corn and she clucked herself over to the front of me and before I knew it, she started pecking on my dress. When she pecked, I screamed. Mama was busy throwing out feed and had not noticed what was happening. She immediately shooed the old hen off and I managed to get worked up into near-hysteria. I was pretty much a scaredy-cat when I was little anyway. After all was calmed down, including me, I decided I hated chickens with a passion from that day forward.

As I grew a little older, I visited my grandparents at their little farm in San Augustine County every summer. I found myself in the chicken yard with Granny. My instructions were to hold the bucket while Granny gathered the eggs from the hen nests. I thought about it and decided I could probably do that since I didn't have any tiny buttons on my dress. We were going about our business, talking about how many eggs we were getting and how we could make some sugar cookies that afternoon, when suddenly Granny reached in a nest and quickly jumped back with a loud "Eek"!

When Granny was scared, I knew I had no business there so I ran to the gate and left her with whatever it was that made her jump. She calmly said to run get Papaw and tell him to bring a hoe. I set the bucket of eggs down, rather bluntly, and started running and yelling. Papaw was down at the barn and, having heard my screaming, was already coming to see what was going on. I told him Granny needed the hoe and him to come. He kind of grinned like it wasn't a big deal, grabbed the hoe, and his long legs didn't take long to get there.

As he got near the gate, he asked Granny, "Is it a snake?"

"Yes," she said, "and he is full of eggs."

I listened to their conversation outside the fence of the chicken yard and held on to the bucket of eggs very tightly.

Granny let Pawpaw come up where he could see in the nest. He looked in and said, "I'm going to lift him out with the hoe handle and then take care of him from there."

"Just don't let him get away. He'll come back tomorrow and get more eggs if you don't kill him," Granny told him.

I ran with the egg bucket as fast as my little short legs would carry me to the back porch and into the house behind the screen door for safety. If there was a chance that snake could get away I didn't want him winding around my leg! Besides that, if he ate eggs he might eat me too. By the time I got behind the screen door and latched it good and tight, Pawpaw had already cut the snake's head off. He looked to see where I was and laughed. Then he said to me, "You want me to get these eggs out of him so you can put them in your bucket?"

It wasn't a bit funny!

THANKSGIVING OF THE 1940S

The road that turned off to Grandmother Nan's worried me. Rain had fallen for days and the white sand mixed with clay was squishy, causing deep ruts as tires made their way down the narrow path. It was more a path than a road, more like a wagon trail. Today we were making our way in the heavy 1948 Dodge coupe. I hated muddy roads. Dad seemed to enjoy seeing how far he could push the car through the mud. The car lurched and stopped.

"We'll have to walk the rest of the way," Dad announced.

My mother looked unhappy but said nothing. Dad grinned as though it were all a game, looked at me, and said, "You're gonna get your shoes muddy." I followed my mother's lead and said nothing. When the door was opened we found ourselves sitting atop sloppy mud, in a very large mud hole.

Mother finally spoke to Dad. "Now we'll have to get all that food out of the turtle hull and carry it the rest of the way." She sounded disgusted.

"Don't worry about the food. You all just go on and watch where you step." Daddy did not seem to get that she was just plain put out by the whole thing.

Mother grabbed my hand and we picked our way out of the mud hole, selecting a higher path to follow to Grandmother Nan's.

The closer we got to the house housing Grandmother Nan, Aunt Ollie, Robbie Lou, and Gloria Jean, we could hear people talking and laughing and loud sounds of joy. I got a whiff of something cooking that flew through the air toward my nose.

"Sure smells good," I grinned up at Mother.

"Grandma's cooking cornbread for the dressing. I've got the old hen cooked in that big pot back there. We're gonna make a big pan o' dressing," she said.

"Will there be any turkey and cake?"

"No turkey, just a big fat hen that came out of our chicken yard. What kind of cake do you want?" she asked.

"A big coconut cake with that calf-slobber frosting," I answered, licking my lips.

"Don't call it that," mother said. "It's called egg-white icing. Your daddy calls it calf slobber, doesn't he?"

I nodded, thinking that was a pretty good description of the fluffy white icing with lots of shredded coconut on top of it, making it look like soft feathers all about.

We arrived to much hugging and kissing. The little house was very small and filled with people. I saw lots of cakes and pies, a big pot of chicken dumplings, and Grandmother Nan bustling about, wiping her hands on her apron. She always made time to hug another grandchild as they came by while stoking the fire in that belching black wood stove.

After what seemed like an awfully long time, she announced dinner was ready. Grandma Nan held up her work-worn arthritic hands to speak before the prayer was offered.

Uncle John spoke in his slow, soft voice. "This is the first dinner since the war [World War II]. Cecil, Virgil, and I left these backwoods and went to that war. Today we are all home from over there and together again. For that we are very thankful." Then he asked my daddy to offer thanks for all those wonderful things.

Nan's big soldier boys gathered her to them while my dad offered thanks. It was truly a wonderful Thanksgiving Day.

THE BATTLE OF NOURNBERG (NUREMBURG)

By Cpl. Cecil F. Veatch

Author's Note: After I'd begged him for quite some time for some story about his service in World War II with General Patton, my uncle Cecil Veatch finally handed me a handwritten story that he hoped would make me leave him alone. Like most soldiers, he did not talk about the war. It haunted him all his life afterward. But his story needs to be told. It represents just one soldier out of thousands who gave it all or whose lives were destroyed by that war. This is copied exactly as he gave it to me, spelling and all. He was indeed a troubled man but he served his country as best he could. He gave it all up for us.

I DO NOT KNOW WHEN all this taken place as we had been marching for three days and time just didn't mean anything to me then. But three days before, we had gotten instructions from General Patton to take the town of Nournberg, Germany. This was our first assignment after rushing the Germans out of France back into Germany. After three days of marching, we finally came to the outskirts of Nournberg. We all were dead on our feet as it was cold and about two feet of snow had done covered the ground.

The old General asked us if we wanted to dig in or take the town and sleep in a fellow bed. What he meant was, we could take the town that night and sleep in their beds. But it wasn't that simple. We had a lot harder time than the General had figured. Being as tired as we were, we just dug in for the night.

The next morning just before dawn, hell broke loose in Nournberg. As we made our first attack, the big brass of the German army had just sat down at the big square table to eat. But they didn't get to eat it at least not then. When they heard that General Patton was in their midst, there was no time for chow. They up and left the table on a run. After taking the town, that is we thought we had it taken, we all gathered up at the same table and was going to eat their meal. But just as we sat down, the Germans made a counterattack and we had to leave. What those officers was doing with a baked ham for breakfast, I never could figure, but there it was big as day. Never had been touched by human hands.

There wasn't much thought about it until we finally taken the town four days later. This battle turned out to be a rough one as we had lost a lot of our men. But what of us was left after it finally ended, gathered up in that same building where we made our first attack. I might add that once again we were cold, tired, and hungry. I don't know whether the German's got to eat their meal or not. But it was all gone and the table was clean.

We were all in a foul mood as it was very cold, well below zero. Some was slouched in chairs, some was laying on the floor, just anywhere we could get out of the cold. Finally, in came old General Patton, corn cob pipe and all. He always carried an old knapsack over his shoulder. He carried it as though it was part of his equipment. He walked up to the table, turned around slowly, looking at every one.

Then he said, "Are you men hungry?"

No one said anything for a moment. Most of us just looked at him like he was a man from mars. Then one guy over in the corner said, "Hell yes, you got anything to eat?"

The General didn't say a word, just kindly taken off his knapsack, taking out the big ham and he slowly turned and counted every man. Then taking out his knife, he cut every man a piece of his choice ham.

P.S. What the General had done when the Germans made their counterattack on us and we had to leave the table, him being the last one to leave, had put the ham in his knapsack and carried it until the battle of Nournberg was finally won.

This is a true statement as written by Cpl. Cecil Veatch, 624th Medical Aid man, U.S. Army, having fought through 5 major battles with General Patton.

THE HANDS

By Andrew Allen Veatch

1900

Author's Note: This poem was written by my great-uncle Andrew Allen Veatch in 1900. When I first read it, I could hardly believe the date on it, but there it was. He was well known in East Texas and Oklahoma Territory as a newspaper man, journalist, and poet. This is amazing for its time.

The brown hand and the white hand
Were clinging close together;
It was in the blooming May-time,
And pleasant was the weather.

There was no one in the garden
To hinder or reprove,
So to the little white hand
The brown declared its love.

The white hand pressed the brown hand,
Warm with passion and with youth.
And made a like confession,
Though quite modestly forsooth.

Communing thus together,
With naught to doubt or dread,
They heeded not how swiftly
The gold-wind'd moments sped.

But at last came time for parting
The precious clasp was riven,
And forth they went by different ways
Under the bright May-heaven.

Ah! Strange perversity of fate,
That overrules us all.
And impotence of Love and Hate,
Immortal, yet how small!

There were after days of brightness,
And days of storm and rain;
But the brown hand and the white hand
Were never linked again.

WAGONS, SLIDES, HORSEBACK, AND WALKING: TRANSPORTATION BACK THEN

Our ancestors came to Texas from somewhere on the Eastern Coast in most cases. They migrated here from England, Germany, Italy, Scotland, and other countries across the Atlantic Ocean. They came by ships and endured severe hardships to get to America. They were escaping from a land of sickness, high taxes, and controlling governments, and from being lorded over by the rich who would never allow them to spread their wings. America was the answer. Many parents sent their children to America even if they could not come themselves because they wanted better opportunities for them. Unless you are an American Indian, you are an immigrant from somewhere in your past.

Many of these immigrants came here with the clothes they had on their backs, a few dollars in their pockets, and a willingness to work from dawn to dusk in order to better their lives. That is where the American work ethic comes from in our histories. Today is much different from the America seen by those ancestors when they stepped off that ship onto American soil. Yet they were so happy to be here. They were willing to put their hand to the plow, or maybe they were blacksmiths, or stonemasons, and wanted to do anything that came before them to eke out a livelihood.

I imagine how it must have been but am not able to create the feelings they would have had on that amazing day they arrived here. My ancestor, James Veatch, arrived here immigrating to England's Maryland Colony in 1651. He was alone and stepped into this country amid a time of political uncertainty.

He sought and received a land grant in Lord Baltimore's plantation while he was still in London. When he arrived here he had holdings of land and the beginning of stature in the colony. In 1653 Veitch was elected as a deputy or what was called an "undersheriff," where he answered to the sheriff for the entire Maryland province. He went on to become "sheriffe," gaining some respect in the colony. But this was all while he was still living under the control of England. King Charles I was beheaded in 1648 but England and Parliament still ruled the colony. It was a difficult time and these early ancestors wanted to get out from under the thumb of England and their reign upon them.

So the first means of travel in early America was horseback or walking. From that time forward until the early years of my grandparents' time that would still be true. Both my grandfathers were farmers. My maternal grandfather never owned any land of his own. He was a sharecropper, working a farm for the owner and getting a very small portion of the goods he raised. He moved his family from farm to farm while seeking a better place to farm and a better owner to work for. He came from northern Louisiana to Texas and settled in Sabine, Shelby, and San Augustine counties. He worked hard plowing the fields with a horse and a mule, loading the corn he raised onto a wagon to transport from the field where it could be dried and made into feed for his animals.

He had only the horse and mule, a few cows for milk and butter, and hogs to butcher in the winter for bacon, ham, and sausage. My grandmother had chickens to provide eggs, and raised smaller fryers for dinner. That is how they made their living up until my grandmother's death in 1957. That is all they knew to do.

Papaw's transportation was the wagon and a slide he built to be pulled by the horse. He used the slide primarily to carry two big barrels to a nearby natural spring where water ran out of the side of a hill. There was a very shallow well at their house but in the summer when the rains stopped and the heat rose, the little well went dry. To get water for his animals and for washing clothes, dishes, and themselves, he loaded the barrels onto the slide and he and the horse went about a half mile to get the water.

He allowed me to go with him sometimes when I was there in the summer. I could ride on the slide all the way to the spring but my firm instructions were that I would have to walk all the way back. Of course, I was more than willing to do that on the way over there but when it was time to come back, I was getting tired. I would beg and plead for him to let me ride on the slide and he would tell me very firmly "no." He never changed his answer, either, no matter how much I whined and pouted. I now understand why. If those big barrels had become unsteady bumbling down that rocky dirt road, they could have topped over on top of me and hurt me. He was not going to have any of that so I had to walk.

Neither grandfather ever owned a car, nor learned to drive. When Papaw Worry needed to go to San Augustine to town to the bank or to the store, he had to walk part of the way. There was a bus that ran daily from Nacogdoches to San Augustine and back later in the day, so Papaw would walk the mile or so from their house down the dirt road to catch the bus. The fare to ride to town and back was minimal. He had to be at the road by about nine o'clock so he could catch his ride to town when the bus would come through their little community. He did his business and was back at the bus station when it ran again in mid-afternoon, going back to Nacogdoches. If he bought much, he had to carry it in his arms while he walked the mile uphill to their house.

Neighbors lived within a half mile of their house, so if they wanted to visit, he and Granny would set off in the afternoon, walking to visit. They had to allow time to get home when it started getting later (like around five o'clock) because the animals all had to be fed, the cows milked, and the eggs gathered. That was life on the little farm. Papaw had a brother who lived probably ten miles away from them, but they rarely saw one another unless they met up in town or on the bus. Ten miles was a long way to walk and taking a wagon would have taken all day to get there, and they would have had to spend the night in order to have much time to visit. They were not able to spend the night unless a close neighbor would go take care of all their animals. Sometimes he did not get to see his brother but once or twice a year and it was only ten miles.

I remember more about my maternal grandfather, Willie George Worry, because he died when I was about nineteen years old. However, my paternal grandfather, Sam Whitson Veatch, died in 1930, before I was born, and I never knew him except through stories I heard about his life.

Sam Whitson Veatch was a relatively tall man with dark black hair. He was the father of nine children with my grandmother, Nan Berryman Veatch. Can you imagine trying to raise a family that large and to feed and clothe them in the early 1900s? Neither can I. Grandmother Nan was a busy lady just trying to keep things going around their house. Sam farmed, hunted game, raised a herd of piney-wood rooters (hogs) for their winter meat, probably killed a deer occasionally, shot wild turkeys and squirrels, and he (like most of the family) loved to fish in McKim Creek or Devil's Ford up in Sabine County where he lived. He worked occasionally, helping someone build a fence, dig a well, or construct a house, including the church house, as well as load pine knots on the little train that took the logs to the sawmills. It is said that he build the little desks they had at the Blackjack School where his children went when they could. He must have been an industrious fellow.

He mostly walked from place to place wherever he needed to go, or went by wagon or maybe horseback. Never owned a car and never knew how to drive one. My, how times have changed!

When you go out today, put the key in the ignition and get that motor to roar for you, back out of your driveway, turn on the heater or air-conditioning, and go on your merry way, do not forget another day. There was a time when those from whom you hail had a little more trouble than that. So prepare to saddle up that big engine you are driving and be thankful to our ancestors for preparing a better way, because that is the way it was.

WASHDAY ON MCKIM CREEK

She had all she could carry trudging down the well-worn trail leading to McKim Creek. The homemade lye soap filled the bag made from a feed sack. It was tucked down into a sheet drawn together by its four corners and filled with dirty clothes. Two of her daughters were coming later carrying more sheets filled with dirty laundry as well. She'd taken the sheet off her and Sam's bed that morning and spread it out on the floor. Then she gathered all the pillowcases and white clothes she could find in her room and tossed them in the middle of the sheet on the floor. Then, gathering its four corners, she threw it over her shoulder for the trek to McKim Creek. It was washday for the Sam Veatch family and Nan Berryman Veatch was on her way to get started. The little woman, standing under five feet tall and the mother of nine children, was tough. It would be a long day filled with the back-breaking work of scrubbing the dirty, sweaty work clothes on a rub-board, leaving bruises on her knuckles. She had the clothes Sam wore as he plowed in the field, sons Pierce and Merlin's work clothes from the Remlig Sawmill, plus dirty socks, pants, and shirts worn by the boys in the family. There was always mending to be done every week. The girls would help her, making the work a little easier. The creek was Nan's wash hole. The black iron washpot sat on the bank waiting.

Chunks of wood from the area were piled up on the creek bank, where a fire would be built under the washpot filled with water from the creek. When the water was hot, it was time to begin doing laundry. It was back-breaking work.

The only blessing of that day and time is that none of them had many clothes to choose from so there were not mounds of clothing belonging to each person in the family. But when there were eleven people in the family, plus sheets and a few thin towels made from feed sacks, the pile grew pretty high. On hot days, even though the washpot was placed strategically on the bank of the creek near the water under thick shade, the breezes stopped and all was still and hot by mid-morning. In the wintertime, they might wait until late morning to begin the ordeal, hoping for the warmest part of the day. Cold northeast wind seemed to pierce the thin clothing they had to wear.

Today it was hot at daybreak, promising a still and humid day. No breeze to stir the thick air around. Even the shade would be hot in a short while. She had on a thin dress made from a feed sack. It had been washed so many times its blue flowers had faded almost white, but the floppy sleeves allowed her to get as much breeze as she could. Her goal was to get the wash done early and hung on the picket fence around the yard back at the house. They would be dry in thirty minutes.

If it had not been so hot, she would have enjoyed the walk to McKim Creek. The birds flew about, chirping loudly, letting all their friends know there was a human on the trail. She smiled as she watched them. She heard something grunting out in the woods and there she glimpsed an armadillo, rooting around a tree looking for something to eat.

She loved the outdoors. Being inside the house and doing housework was not her favorite thing. She loved the garden, being out in the woods with her beloved Sam. The kids all ran every which way every day, with the older ones taking care of the younger ones when they were small.

Now they were mostly all grown. Some had left home and some were back and forth. She never knew how many would show up for supper every night.

Reaching the opening at the creek, she saw two deer getting a drink at the creek bank. She stopped to watch. What a beautiful sight, she thought. But work awaited her and she approached the washpot, watching the deer sprint away. She had brought some rich lighter pine pieces to start her fire and she set to work laying the pine, lighting it, and adding some bigger chunks of wood to the fire. One of her sons had come down before her and filled the pot with water from the creek. That helped.

A homemade table stood near the washpot. There she laid the dirty clothes. Nearby, the two galvanized round tubs sat filled with water that would be used to rinse the lye soap out of the clothes after they boiled in the washpot of hot water. She got her battling stick (stirring stick) from atop the table, and with her pocketknife she chipped the lye soap into small chunks and tossed them in the smoking-hot water. It began to melt from the heat and she added as many sheets as the pot would allow without running over, stirring gradually around and around with the battling stick. She saw that she would have two pots of white clothes and towels. It made her back hurt.

She heard Hattie, her oldest daughter, and Viola, the next in line, fussing at one another as they came down the trail. "Lord, what am I going to do with those two," she thought, "they just flat don't like each other," as she raised her voice to them, saying, "We'll have none of that today. There's too much to do down here."

They quieted down, although Viola was sporting a full-fledged pout when they arrived. The laundry process began in silence. Hattie had such a sweet nature, Nan thought, and never spoke back when Viola was ugly to her. Maybe if she stood up to her more it would be good for Viola. The problem was, Viola was Sam's favorite girl and the rest of the children knew it. Nan was not sure how to handle this, since Sam was pretty hard-headed about his children.

The work went on. Stirring, rinsing out the lye soap, scrubbing stains on the rub board, wringing out the clothing as best they could, and taking them back to the house to hang on the picket fence around the home place. This back-breaking work went on all morning long.

As the sun moved to almost directly over them, signifying that it was noon, they were able to empty the tubs and the washpot, turning them upside down to keep them as clean as possible until next wash day.

"What are we going to have for lunch?" Viola asked in her demanding voice.

"I put on a pot of dry pintos with a ham hock in them before I left the house. They should be about ready and we'll have the leftover cornbread from last night," Hattie said quietly.

"I hate pintos and cornbread," Viola snipped.

Nan spoke. "Well, I guess you'll just have to scramble you an egg or something because that is all there is."

They slowly made their way to the house to finish hanging out the last of the wash and take down the sheets and pillowcases that were now dry. Nan told Hattie to go check on lunch and she and Viola would hang out the rest of the clothes. Needless to say, Viola didn't like those rules and stomped about like a mad old cow. There would only be the womenfolk and the youngest children for lunch since everyone else was working or had already moved away from the home place.

When the clothes were dealt with, Nan and Viola went inside and Hattie had the lunch on the wooden table with bowls for each of them and had rounded up the twins, Murry and Cecil, and the youngest girl, Ollie. As they sat down to eat, Sam came in from his job in the woods, where he had been loading pine knots on the mill trains that were hauling the big virgin timber to the sawmills. Immediately, Viola ran to him and began her whining tattle about how hard they had made her work all morning.

Sam caught the look from Nan and knew he'd best not comment so he washed his hands and sat down for lunch. Sometimes, after a hard morning's work, it was just best to let things alone and eat what you had before you. At least that was what they all did, including Viola, who didn't like pinto beans and cornbread.

WASHING DISHES WAY BACK WHEN

WAY BACK IN THE '50S when a meal was over, usually some of the kids were appointed by the lady of the house to do the dishes. Now, that did not mean rinse, load in the dishwasher, push the button, and go on about your business. No, that meant put some water on the stove in a kettle to boil, clean off the table and stack the dirty dishes, rake out the scraps into the hog slop, and get out a dishpan to wash dishes and a rinsing pan to rinse the dishes. Lay out clean dishtowels to dry with. When all that is together, the kettle with hot water will be whistling, ready to pour into the dishpan, and the process begins. Cool it down slightly with some water dipped from the water bucket used for drinking water.

My job was always to dry and put away. My great delight was to find a glass or cup that my cousin, who washed, had not gotten completely clean. I got to send it back and say, "Unclean!" That usually resulted in a lot of muttering and whining from the dish-washer person, probably because I got such delight in doing it.

Dishes were washed with a tool we called a "dish rag." This item was usually an old dishtowel that had gotten worn out and was torn into two pieces and finished its life as a dish rag. We used homemade lye soap, crumbled in pieces into the dishpan with the hot water poured over it. It melted and made the soap we needed to clean our dishes. We had no Dawn, Palmolive, or any such soap, nor Cascade for our machine that would wash dishes. It took a little while to wash dishes after a big family dinner. We had no paper plates either. China plates were used, usually not matching designs, but whatever had been passed down from family to family. Sometimes foods like oatmeal would have little juice-type glasses in their boxes, and all of those were used for the children. Most dishes, if they were new, were ordered from the Sears Roebuck or Montgomery Ward catalog that every home cherished.

The best thing about washing dishes was the conversation in the kitchen. It took time to do the task and our mothers were busy putting away the food that was left, wiping off the oilcloth on the big wooden dining table, sweeping under the table, and talking. Kids were not usually allowed to listen to grown-up conversations back then. Our job was to be outside playing or doing chores we were assigned. So the chore of washing dishes allowed us to listen in on our mother's conversations with cousins, sisters, and aunts that might be around in the kitchen. We would get very quiet when we realized they were talking about something we wanted to hear. Maybe it was about a neighbor whose housekeeping lacked the finesse they felt was necessary, or maybe some woman from church did not dress appropriately for church, maybe some woman was about to have a baby and was having some problems. Yes, it was community gossip, and our ears perked up like you would not believe.

Occasionally we heard information about our family history if our grandma was there. She might talk about where they used to live and how hard life was for farmers back then. How their mother and father came by wagons from Mississippi or some place that seemed foreign to us, and how one of the babies died on the way. We learned bits and pieces of a lot of things about life as we washed and dried dishes.

As our chore was ending, we got a little playtime in as the dishwasher began thumping water on the dish-dryer. Of course, the dish-dryer started popping the dish-washer with the wet dishtowel and the fight was on until our mothers spotted us and stopped that fun quickly. There always seemed to be an adult around to stop our fun!

Washing dishes was a chore that even then was not difficult to do. When I remember how much we learned about life while washing and drying dishes, I think that children today are missing out. They don't have to wash dishes like we did and they miss out on conversations because they do not happen anymore. I am thankful for my dishwasher that is electric and all I have to do is load it, put some detergent in it, and push a button. It does the work. But my kids did not even have to load it. I did. They missed that conversation about life and family. This is just one of the few times in my life that I enjoyed getting to listen to family talk about their lives before me that were gone. I am thankful for that pleasure of washing dishes, listening, and enjoying the women who went before me.

WHAT? NO TV? NO A/C? NO ELECTRICITY?

"You kids get out of this house!" Mama said with a wave of her broom.

Nobody argued with Mama if they had good sense.

Kids back in the '40s and '50s knew if one spoke back or whined when given this order, there was a heavy list of chores waiting for them. Youngsters made their way out the front door in a hurry.

"You kids get out from under my feet or I'm going to give you plenty to do!" Mama said. This was a saying we did not like to hear either. There was no television to watch and getting out of Mama's sight as quickly as possible was always a good idea.

Later on, in the early 1960s, we got a big boxy black-and-white television with rabbit ears and an antenna outside the house to watch when we were allowed. Our television was not turned on during the day until 12:30 p.m., when Mama sat down in her favorite rocking chair with a glass of iced tea, demanding quiet. If a child could not be quiet, they were sent outside at once, because it was time for *As The World Turns* and nothing and nobody interfered with that.

Summers in the 1940s and '50s were as hot as blazes inside and outside. There was no air-conditioning in houses then, either. Doors and windows were wide open and if we had screens keeping out the bug, wasps, and mosquitoes, we considered ourselves quite "up-town" folk.

There were screen doors protecting the doorways from these pesky bugs and the doors were held shut with a spring that was hooked to the door facing the screen door. If one was running and allowed that door to slam, oh my! That's when a loud and clear voice could be heard demanding that you "come back and close that door right." I can still hear that voice in my head.

Most houses were built with a long front and back porch. These were not so much for appearances as for doing work, resting, or visiting. Many bushels of purple hull peas were shelled on such a porch early in the morning when it was a bit cooler. Bushels of corn were shucked and prepared for canning on the front or back porch as well. Potatoes were peeled, saws were filed to make them sharper, and yarns were told to little ears there on the porch. It was a grand place for work, tales, and yarns, and for education. Much family history was shared on the front porch. The neighbors passing by, seeing a family out on the porch, took time to stop by to chat for a while. They talked about politics, religion, families, and the days gone by.

After the work was done, it was the place the women who worked all day, canning the food for wintertime use, came to sit down and rest a bit. As darkness eased its inky blackness into the yard, it was time for play as well. We had pea hull fights, which can be described as chasing one another with pea hulls while telling a girl cousin that there was a big worm on your pea hulls. Then screaming was the exact reaction expected and desired.

We chased fireflies, which we called "lightnin' bugs," collecting them in jars so we could watch them light up the darkness that surrounded us. We were told to be quiet for a moment so we could listen to the whippoorwill deep in the big woods calling a mate.

Bedtime came early on days like that. The grown-ups were tired and would have to get up early the next morning to continue the canning procedure over again. Granny would say, "Time to go to bed. We've got to can tomatoes tomorrow." Of course we begged to stay a little longer, but it didn't work back then like I see it work with kids today.

Parents tell their kids three, four, maybe five times to do something today, and they just keep right on doing what they're doing without flinching or making a move to obey. That did not happen in the '40s and '50s, at least not at our house. If Granny spoke or Mama spoke and we didn't listen and start moving in the direction we were instructed, the next thing I remember hearing was a deeper-toned voice.

It would say, "I thought your grandmother told you to get ready for bed."

I would quickly answer, "Yes sir."

WHAT I LEARNED FROM MY DADDY

Murry Veatch was born about five miles east of Brookeland, Texas (Sabine County), in 1915 to Sam and Nan Veatch. He was not born alone. He had a twin brother born with him named Cecil. Dad was forever a mischievous kid who loved to laugh and have fun. He was what I would call a fun dad, except when I got into some kind of trouble of which he did not approve. Then he could get real serious very quickly. I had a healthy respect for him for that and many other reasons.

I learned early on that being the only child in the family had its perks, but it also had its problems. When trouble came along, I had no siblings to blame it on. It was always my fault. That got to be a problem that I did not enjoy. Although he had my best interests at heart, he had high expectations for me, his only child.

Dad was a relatively short fellow, squarely built, tough as could be and a hard worker. As a young man, he worked at whatever he could find to bring in a little money for him and Mama and my grandmother, who lived with them. His brothers went to serve in World War II and he was left to take care of Grandma. He worked at Temple Lumber Company building bomb crates for the war.

When the war was over, he worked in the Dimension Plant at Temple a total of eleven years before moving the family to Jasper, where he became an employee of the Texas Department of Highways. There he retired. Daddy loved to raise a big garden. We canned or put in the freezer all we could use and he gave away the rest. Many sacks of potatoes, tomatoes, peas, and corn came out of that big garden as long as he could farm. He was a giving, caring person.

I learned many things from Daddy, and these are just a few of them.

1. **Work at something until you can find something better.** In the early years of the Great Depression, he helped dig water wells by hand, built fences for neighbors, drove his old uncle's car to take him places, worked in sawmills, and finally patched holes in the highways.
2. **Have a little fun along the way.** This was important to him. He had a streak of mischief in him a mile long and loved playing practical jokes on everyone from his mother to the men who worked with him. One did not play checkers with him because he always won. You did not play forty-two dominoes with him, either. He used to tell his grandsons when playing dominoes, "If you're not cheating, you're not trying," when they accused him of little under-the-table tricks.
3. **Love your mate with all your heart and be careful when you choose one.** There was never any doubt in my mind that he loved Mother. He bought her things he wanted her to have to make her life easier.
4. **Serve the Lord with whatever you have.** He did that by giving away vegetables out of his garden without ever charging a dime to anyone for them. He worked on the hot or cold highways all day and afterward went to the church, building and worked on the parking lot. He served as Deacon for many years.
5. **Take better care of your health than I did.** He notoriously would not eat healthy foods. He was raised very poor and when

he got all the food he wanted in his home, he saw no need to deprive himself any more. When he developed diabetes late in life, we found packages of Honey Buns on his table one day. His grandson, Jason, asked him what they were doing there. He replied, "Oh, I got them for the dog." Sure enough.

6. **Make kids mind and show respect.** I got into more trouble for "sassing" him back than anything else. He would not tolerate a smart-mouthed kid, and yet he had one!
7. **Take care of and respect the elderly.** He did many things for my grandmother, his mother, his blind sister, and my mother-in-law to make their lives easier out of his respect for the elderly. His mother lived with us many years, finally passing away at our home in Holly Springs.
8. **Travel a little.** He loved going on vacation with Mother's brother and sister-in-law every spring. They usually went to Arkansas or Branson, Missouri, for about a week, and he had a blast.
9. **Always smile.** Nobody wants to look at a sour face. He used to tell me that when I was mad and pouting about something. It never worked on him.
10. **Don't ever quit. Always keep trying.** He believed in keeping on until you got it right. He worked hours and hours on old lawn mowers and his old Farmall tractor, trying to get them to work. He did not quit until he succeeded either.

He always liked the old hymn "Beautiful Life" and would sing it while working on something outside. I could hear him many times, singing, "Each day I'll do a golden deed, by helping those who are in need. My life on earth is but a span and so I'll do the best I can." And he did.

WHAT I LEARNED FROM GRANNY WORRY

My maternal grandmother was a worthy woman. Every thought and memory I have of her reminds me of Proverbs 31:10–31. Today many will say that no woman is really that good, and in today's world, there may be very few. Evie Rains Worry was born and raised in Shelby County, Texas, in 1887 and died June 3, 1952. She was a woman of noble character, worth far more than rubies, who supported her husband all the days of her life, arose while it was still dark, and provided food for her family. She set about her work vigorously with strong arms, helped those that she could, made numerous quilts for her family, and was clothed with strength and dignity. All these things truly fit her spirit. Granny passed away on my fourteenth birthday, a day I shall never forget. Although I did not have her long in my life, she made a profound impression on my soul, my actions, and my spirit. I miss her terribly even now, over sixty years later.

What did I learn from her is hard to encapsulate in this tribute. Granny's reward should be great because of all the good she did in her life. She lived in the time where women wore dresses down to their ankles. She made all her clothes on her Singer Treadle Sewing Machine. Any other clothing she may have needed, she ordered from Sears Roebuck's mail-order catalog.

She cooked on a wood stove that was contrary and made her kitchen stifling hot in summer when she was canning food for the winter. In the winter, the stove made her kitchen nice and cozy warm. Her once dark-brown hair was white as snow and when combed out at night, it came down to her waist. She wore it gathered into a thick bun at the nape of her neck. Her teeth were removable and she wore high-top sneakers for her work days at home.

Here are some lessons she taught me:

1. **Be thankful for whatever you have every day.** She did not have much in the way of "things" that we take for granted today. She did not have running water in her house. She did not have inside bathrooms. She did have a sturdy little two-bedroom farmhouse that kept them warm and safe. And she was thankful.
2. **Work, for the night is coming when man's work is o'er.** She sang that old song while working in her kitchen many times. I often wondered if she was looking forward to the day when her work would be over and she could rest.
3. **Always be honest and truthful**. Believe me, she did not like for me to lie to her. I tried it once and it did not work out too well for me.
4. **Don't complain.** Work with joy in your heart. She did.
5. **Be thankful for your family and good friends.** She sold eggs to some folks for a few pennies to go in her egg-money jar, but if someone could not pay, she just gave them away. She sold milk and butter as well for the money jar and then she gave more of it away to someone who needed it. Her heart was soft and pure.
6. **Life is not about how much you have but how much you give.** Today we hear people say they don't have the money to help someone. Many times, money is not what they need. Granny had no money to speak of but when a need arose, she always

found a way to feed them, or give them a quilt for the winter or milk to drink. Birthday gifts to me from Granny and Papaw Worry were usually twenty-five cents. Not much, you think. It came out of her egg-money jar and I never knew it was not much. It made me happy.

7. **Study and learn what God wants you to do.** She read her Bible at night by the light of the kerosene lamp, sitting in the fireplace room, and she and Papaw talked about whatever she was reading. Study and learn.
8. **Keep yourself pure in God's sight.** She cautioned us grandkids about that often. At the time I was not too sure of what it meant exactly, but since I was the only girl, she often cautioned me about behavior around the opposite sex. She wanted me to be good and proper.
9. **Do not gossip about family or neighbors.** She often told me that we should be careful how we spoke of others. Maybe she knew I was going to need that one pretty bad!
10. **Be a worker for the Lord and He will be with you.** She liked to sing the old hymn "I Want to be a Worker for the Lord" as she worked. There may have been a lot of things she did not understand, and if she came back today she would be appalled. The way people dress, the things we watch on television, and the way people talk would embarrass her. Upsetting would not be the word for it. She would be sitting her family down with that old King James Version of the Bible on her lap, resting on her apron, and we would have an old fashioned "set to"!

I adored Granny. I didn't have her but fourteen years, so never believe you are not able to influence your grandchildren in a short period of time. She did. I think of her often and will be so happy to see her when I get to heaven. What a reunion it will be!

WHAT I LEARNED FROM MY MOTHER

My mother was born in 1916 in Shelby County, Texas. Her parents were farmers and her schooling was through the eleventh grade. She was smart, but all hands were needed to help make the crops in those days. When planting time came in the spring, she was needed at home. School had to wait. The only way she could finish high school was by boarding in San Augustine with someone or riding a bus there every day. There was no money for her to do either, so she only went through the eleventh grade at the little country school in Denning, Texas. She always regretted that. She always wanted to graduate high school and I wish she had later, but she never thought she could.

When she married my daddy, at age twenty, she moved to Brookeland, Texas, to live. There she continued to help farm, keep house, and cook for whoever was at the home place at that time. Shortly after I was born, they moved to Pineland, Texas, where they were able to rent a little shotgun millhouse while Daddy worked at Temple Lumber Company.

After eleven years of that, they moved to Jasper, where Daddy went to work for the Texas Department of Transportation and Mother worked in the lunchroom at Jasper schools. They were finally able to get enough together to buy a little two-bedroom house in Holly Springs along with three acres of land. It did not look like much but eventually Daddy built a new house. They were always working hard and trying to better themselves. Life was not easy.

I have thought long and hard about what things I learned from Mama. This is the most difficult one to write because she poured so much of herself into me and my life. She taught me things every day by her example. She believed in me and encouraged me in every opportunity she could. So these are just a few of the things she left embedded in me.

1. **Cleanliness is next to godliness.** She repeated that to me so many times I can still hear her say it. I was kind of a sloppy kid and did not really have time to pay attention to that cleanliness stuff. But you could have eaten off Mama's floors, whether they were wood or faded linoleum.
2. **Trust in the Lord with all your might.** Her example taught me that on a daily basis.
3. **Honesty is the best policy.** She did not believe in lying to her. One day I decided to go visit the neighbors without telling her. They were having a pretty good-looking supper so I just decided to stay and eat with them. The lady asked me if Mama knew where I was and I readily replied "yes." When Mama found me with that little peach-tree switch in her hand and swatted my legs all the way home, I realized that lying to Mama was not too good of an idea.
4. **Patience is a virtue. Quiet time is good.** Neither of those elements fit into my personality very well. If I had been smart, I would have adjusted better to them, knowing they were quite important to Mama. But, as you can tell, I was not that smart.
5. **Family is important. Take care of it.** We had a big extended family then. Daddy had six living siblings as I was growing up, plus their families. Mama had one brother and his family, so cousins, aunts, and uncles were important in my life, and they

all contributed to my attitudes in many instances.

6. **Help people any way you can.** I wish I knew how many pies, cakes, pots of peas and beans, pones of cornbread, and plates of fried chicken Mama carried and gave to people in need. It would be amazing. You understand, she did not run down to the local Brookshire Brothers and buy this food. She cooked it from scratch and most of it came from her garden and her chicken house. When she visited the sick, she took food. When someone died, she took food. Food was going to make everybody better in her eyes. I think it did, too.

7. **Study to show yourself approved to God.** Mama taught Bible classes of first graders through fourth graders for over fifty years. She told me one time that she was teaching the third generation of children in some families. She believed in teaching children about Jesus, about the Old Testament stories that are there for our review and learning. She was an awesome teacher.

8. **Laugh and love.** She could not have been married to my daddy for over sixty years and not believed that. She loved her grandsons with all her heart and was known to dance a jig when report cards came in and they were pleasing to her. She had a song she made up and sang when she scrambled their eggs for them as well. Her laughter and her joy were contagious.

9. **Enjoy the beauty of the earth.** She especially had a knack for growing flowers. She loved roses dearly and pampered them so that she had a beautiful garden of them in her yard. I can still see her late in the evening when the sun was still very hot, outside with her water hose, wearing her old dress and her bonnet as she touched and watered each one of her precious flowers.

10. **Philippians 4:11 "I have learned the secret of being content in any and every situation…"** This is the scripture she quoted me

one Sunday morning as she was dying from cancer and everyone had gone to church but the two of us. I was reading to her out of the Bible and I read this scripture. I asked her if she ever wondered why she got the cancer. She looked at me very straight and hard and replied with the quote of Philippians 4:11. There was no doubt in my mind that she had it all figured out in her muddled brain that was being destroyed by the terrible disease.

When I think of her today, I recall one night shortly before she passed away and I was staying with her on a little bed beside her in her bedroom. She was having some pain from the brain cancer by then and I had given her something for it. I was trying to help her relax and go to sleep. Somehow it seemed appropriate to sing old church songs to her, one after another, yet she remained restless. I held her hand and finally I sang, "When peace like a river attendeth my way. When sorrows like sea billows roll. Whatever my lot thou has taught me to say, It is well, it is well with my soul." I felt her hand relax in mine as she went to a restful sleep. I know that indeed it was well with her soul. I will always miss her but the teachings and examples she left by her example before me will abide with me as long as I am here on this earth. I love you, Mama.

WHAT I LEARNED FROM PAPAW WORRY

My maternal grandfather, Willie George Worry, was a farmer. He was born in Louisiana in 1891 and migrated across the Sabine River in the early 1900s with his parents and siblings. He was educated through about the fifth grade before he was compelled to leave school to help with the farm.

Papaw was a tall, lanky fellow whose long strides were difficult for my short legs to keep up with, but he let me tag along after him as often as he could. He was not a very talkative fellow and he spoke indistinctly with a low, muttering kind of voice. Usually he dressed in blue overalls with a blue chambray shirt and always wore a black felt hat. He was a good man and went through life having never owned any property of his own, never driven anything but a wagon and plow horses. He lived simply in a simple time.

But he taught me a lot of things as I grew up, and I want to share some of these things I remember that might help some younger person understand the way it was.

1. **If a man does not work, he does not eat.** This comes from II Thessalonians 3:10, but his example taught me that he believed that with all his heart. He worked hard and had very little time off, but he was a faithful Christian man.

2. **Toil the earth and it will provide for you.** As a farmer, he understood the concept of planting and reaping the harvest. He believed that if a person worked hard, planted, and hoed, God gave the increase. That was all he wanted in his life. To take care of family and to share with others.
3. **Observe nature. It will teach you.** He was an "outside" man. His life revolved around taking care of his animals, his farm, and things that needed repair around his little farm. No, he did not have many material things from our viewpoint today, but he had many things that we do not have today. He took time to watch the clouds, the birds, the cows and horses, and all things in God's creation. They were part of his day every day.
4. **Work all day, every day but Sunday.** That is the Lord's Day. He observed that faithfully.
5. **Life is hard. Put your hand to the plow.** He did not cotton to folks who did not work to make their way. He worked very hard for very little in a monetary sense and people who were not willing to do that might get a bit of his ire at times.
6. **Be a Christian in all you do.** I don't remember really seeing him angry many times at all. He took it all in stride, and if you've ever plowed with a Georgia stock and a horse and mule, you know that could try one's patience. I have seen him frustrated and have heard him speak sharply to the team while plowing, but he never did it to me, Granny, or the other grandkids. I'm sure we deserved it sometimes.
7. **Patience and faith.** "All I know is farming," he would say. "Plowing behind a horse and mule, planting, hoeing, weeding, and harvesting. Then starting all over again."
8. **"Be strong and of good courage"** comes to my mind when thinking about him. He would have liked Joshua of old, as he

repeatedly told the Israelites that over and over again.

9. **You have to give back to others and they will help you when you need it.** Obey the law and do what's right. He sat in his straight-backed wooden chair on cold winter nights before the popping fireplace, his long legs stretched out before him, and rolled his Prince Albert cigarette. Those words about helping others were part of his thinking as he rested and spoke of a neighbor who was having a harder time than he. Willie Worry shared with them some of that pork he had smoking in his smokehouse so they would have food for their children.

10. **Do what's right.** He would be amazed at the things going on in our world today. He would be concerned about his great-great-grandchildren and the things they are dealing with in a world he knew nothing about.

I am so glad I had him in my life and grateful for the things he taught me, some by his words but most by his actions. Thank you, Papaw Worry, for your simple knowledge.

SUMMER PLACE

I remember my summer place
Soft breezes gently touching my face.
I remember feeling the soft red sand
So cool and silky in my hand.
The days were bright with joy and fun
I never once noticed the sun.
Corn stalks rustled as the breeze went by
Birds chirped happily in the sky.
My own little world lived there in my mind
In my place of peace and nothing unkind.
My knees were dirty through and through
My heart was clean like the morning dew.
There in my soul where I grew up from a child
Learned about nature and things worthwhile.
Those times are gone and can ne'er be replaced,
Because they are still there in my summer place.

This sums up my memories of the way it was. Most of these memories are from fifty or sixty years ago, yet they are still vivid in my mind. This is the reason I am who I am and have become what I have become today. As you read these stories and think on these poems, I hope you have some special "summer place" in your past that makes your days brighter and guides you along life's way. I know I'm very thankful for mine.

ABOUT THE AUTHOR

ALENE DUNN ENJOYS WRITING ABOUT growing up in East Texas and about the people who lived there. She has long been an avid genealogist and has followed her family history of those who came to this area in the early 1800s, paving the way for development of these forests. Her wish is to cherish these stories and never let these memories die by passing them on to others. She hopes these stories will touch her readers in some way, bringing back precious memories.

She is an active member of the Daughters of the Republic of Texas, the Daughters of the American Revolution, and the Jasper Church of Christ. She has two sons and two granddaughters. She has published one book (Red Dirt and Sand Hill Stories), writes family history, scrapbooks, teaches ladies Bible Class, is an avid reader, and loves spending time with her family.

She would love to hear from you with comments at dunnmom2004@yahoo.com